The Quiet Spirits

Ann Edall-Robson

FriesenPress

Suite 300 - 990 Fort St
Victoria, BC, V8V 3K2
Canada

www.friesenpress.com

First Edition — 2017

The Quiet Spirits is a work of fiction. Names, characters, businesses, places, events and incidents are either the products of the author's imagination or used in a fictitious manner. Any resemblance to actual persons, living or dead, or actual events is purely coincidental.

Steven W. West - Consultant

Leon Strembitsky - Author Photograph

Ann Edall-Robson (DAKATAMA) - Book Cover Photograph

ISBN
978-1-5255-1160-8 (Hardcover)
978-1-5255-1161-5 (Paperback)
978-1-5255-1162-2 (eBook)

1. FICTION, CONTEMPORARY WOMEN

Distributed to the trade by The Ingram Book Company

Dedication

It is where I come from that draws me to where I need to go. Capturing moments others may never get to experience. Sharing an era many will not know. Ranching, farming, small towns and gravel roads are the backbone of our nation.

Thank you to all who embrace and live the traditions and lifestyle of our western heritage.

~1~

Looking down at the words on the page, Brandi Westeron finished her coffee. Flipping the book shut, she walked out of the kitchen.

Today being Saturday, the local bakery would have their breakfast special on: two pieces of French toast, made with thick slices of bread from their own ovens, served with a choice of two slices of home-grown bacon or homemade sausage, and a never-ending cup of coffee. Who could pass up a meal for $6.99, especially when it came with the possibility of much more?

Brandi had discovered the Saturday morning gatherings to be a treasure house of local folklore, stories, and colourful clientele. They had accepted her as one of their own, when she moved to Notclin several years before. The locals took as much pride in her writing as she did, always inquiring about what she was working on and for which publications. It gave them bragging rights to outsiders, the out-of-towners who made the trek from the city in search of the Saturday special for themselves.

Opening the door to The Bakery, Brandi waved hello to owner Marnee Cranworth. The slightly built lady, who always wore her greying hair in a twist knot at her neck, lifted her hand in a greeting.

"Here to have the special or just a coffee this morning?"

"I'll have the special, please." Brandi headed towards the corner table, where a man wearing a cowboy hat was sitting.

She enjoyed Pete's company and liked to sit with him whenever they were there at the same time. He could be found at the same table, sipping a coffee and quietly watching everything that was going on. He always had a friendly smile for everyone. Why he had befriended Brandi was a mystery, but she thanked her lucky stars he had.

Pete had been instrumental in providing her with information when she'd written the Western Homesteads article for the *Homestead Life Quarterly* magazine. She had given him the recognition he deserved as a source reference, introducing him to the world outside this sleepy little town, as P. C. Noll, advisor. To her, and everyone in Notclin, he was just Pete.

This Saturday would be different from others they'd spent together at that table. They would talk about the weather, local sports, and news, migrating to the occasional bit of political spice, thrown in to step it up a bit. Today, Brandi knew there would be more to discuss than the general small talk they were used to.

Pete watched the young woman sitting across from him, eating her breakfast. He hadn't said much since she'd sat down, but that wasn't uncommon either, as they sometimes sat for quite a time contemplating their own thoughts. He finally leaned back in his chair, pushed his hat back on his head, stretched his long legs out under the table, and crossed his arms on his chest.

"What's on your mind?"

"Well, Pete," she said, between swallowing her food and taking a drink of coffee, "I've had a dream. I guess not one. A few—heck, more than a few."

Pete chuckled and sat up in his chair, leaning his elbows on the table.

"We all have dreams, girl. What's so special about yours that has you eating one of Marnee's full breakfasts? Or didn't you notice she didn't give you your regular half order?"

Brandi looked down at her plate. Pete was right, and she was stuffed. She pushed the plate off to the side and reached for Pete's empty cup.

They were both going to need a refill for what she had to tell him. She picked up the cups and made her way across the room to the coffee pot. Only in a small town could she get her own coffee in a cafe.

Settling back in the chair opposite Pete, Brandi set the cups on the table. This wasn't going to be easy for her. She worked best when she had a plan, an outline, or at least a semi-final vision of what the result would be. The light at the end of the tunnel of the myriad of research she usually compiled.

She had to remember that this was like writing, digging in places she needed to know more about. A journey to somewhere and back to get the answer and share the findings. The difference? This was about her personally, making it strange ground for her.

"So you had a dream?" Pete asked, lifting his cup to his mouth.

Brandi nodded, fidgeting with her napkin. Pete had never seen her quite this unsettled. Her professional composure was gone. She was like a kid that had been caught with her hand in the cookie jar.

He slowly let out a breath. "Let's have it before you implode."

"I don't really know where to start. There's been these dreams, and it's like I'm being sucked in, or driven to do or find something. There isn't much to go on."

Brandi took a drink of her coffee. Setting the mug down, she looked square into Pete's eyes. She knew she could trust him. He wouldn't laugh at her or her thoughts.

"After I finished the homestead piece, I vegged for a bit. I didn't want to jump right into another heavy-load project and the editors understood. I have a few deadlines I'm working on but nothing unusual. Easy-ride stuff."

Pete nodded and looked towards the door as it opened. Smiling, he waved to the couple entering. He felt the need to keep things normal and simple during this story time Brandi was sharing with him. There was something in her voice that he couldn't put a finger on, but it was making him uneasy.

"So you took some down time?" he said, bringing his attention back the woman sitting across from him. "Everybody needs that in their life. A time to take stock and revisit their dreams. Even you, Miss Got-to-Getter-Done!"

She laughed. He had called her that on a few occasions when she was serious and bogged down.

"I didn't say I revisited my dreams. I said I had one. Rather, I've had at least two recently that are bugging me, and I am sure they are related."

"What were they about?"

"That's just it; I don't really know."

"We're having a conversation about your dreams. You don't know what they are about, but you think they are related."

Pete started to get up. He didn't know where this was heading, but until she could come up with more material, he couldn't see the sense of the exchange. They might just as well be talking about the weather or some other inconsequential topic.

She put a hand on his arm.

"Sit down, please, and listen to my jabber. I think you will agree with me that the dreams could easily belong together, but they happened a few weeks apart."

"All right," he said, sitting. "When did the first dream happen?"

"After I finished the homestead article."

"What stands out in your mind about these dreams?"

"A meadow."

"That's it? A meadow? Nothing more? No people, no buildings, no other scenery?"

"Nope. Well, a long meadow and not being there by myself. I get this niggling feeling there's more to this," She said sheepishly. "I thought it was just my mind clearing the residue from the last year's research. Then about two weeks later, I had another dream."

"Tell me about the second dream."

Pete was interested only because he knew Brandi would not have come to him if she didn't think it was important. The thought of spending a Saturday morning listening to nothingness wasn't something he enjoyed. For her, he would sit. For her, he would listen. She was one person he would help in a heartbeat.

"I can't remember any particular part of the dream. It was pretty much like the first one. Does that sound crazy to you?"

A low, muffled guffaw escaped his lips. "It sounds down right ludicrous. Whatever you have been eating or drinking before you go to bed, you had better stop. Like you said, maybe it's just your mind clearing the cobwebs left behind from your boxes of research."

He finished the last of his coffee and set the cup beside the plate at the back of the table.

"What are your plans? Are you going to let this go? Chalk it up to just what they are: dreams? Or are you going to spend all your free time chasing the unknown?"

Brandi was crestfallen. For some reason, she thought Pete would be more supportive. She actually thought he would give her some answers. Something, anything, so she could go along her merry way, leaving the dreams behind.

"I've already gone through my research boxes to see if it was one of the places I'd visited for the Western Homesteads piece, or someplace you and I talked about. Nothing! I can't help feeling there is more to this, and it's important, Pete. I'd like your help in trying to decipher it."

"I'd like to help, girl, but you aren't giving me a lot to go on. Why don't you give it some time? Maybe you'll have another dream. Make some more notes on what you do or don't remember and then give me a call if you come up with anything."

He got up, and as he walked past her he lay his hand on her shoulder.

"It'll come together for you. You know it always does."

With that, he left Brandi to sort through her thoughts.

~2~

Talking with Pete had not set Brandi's mind at ease. She'd come away with a determination she often possessed when thrown into a deadline dilemma, only this time it was her subconscious driving her to find the answers.

Days of mapping out a plan, going for drives, making notes, and ignoring her commitments all came to a grinding halt when she received a call from one of the magazine editors she worked with, asking if she was ill. She had never missed a conference call before, and he was concerned for her health.

Embarrassed, Brandi couldn't stop apologizing to the man who, over the years, had trusted her dependability and her work. He'd made a point of telling her that her input was not only important but also needed on the team project in which she was involved in. After the conversation ended, the realization that her dream fixation had to stop was more than evident. It was time to focus on the fork in the road that led back to normal.

She smirked when she thought of her form of normal. It started early, with her first cup of coffee, leaning against the kitchen counter and watching the sun come up over the trees. This is where she planned her days, filled with writing, hours of research, and some domestic chores thrown in to allow her brain some breathing room.

Standing in the kitchen on this particular day, Brandi's morning planning session skidded into the ditch. Pete had been right; she was no further ahead than the day he told her she had nothing to go on. She had let the dreams start to consume her every waking moment.

The revelation that life needed to go on had a calming effect on Brandi. She busied herself cleaning up the breakfast dishes. A look out the window confirmed it would be a good day to get outside. A walk would clear away some of the fluff from her mind.

The best place to start, she decided, was a walk to the post office at the other end of town. She'd sent out some query letters the previous month, and it would be about time for responses to start trickling in.

With thoughts on work, Brandi wanted to be home by early afternoon. Filling her backpack with a notebook, camera, and a small thermos of water, she was more than ready to get out into the fresh air. Knowing she worked best with a plan, she outlined her walk in her mind. Take a stroll through the downtown to see what and who was new in her part of the world. Lunch at The Bakery would tie in with a visit with Marnee. Seeing Marnee would be a great way to end her outing.

The team report, she promised herself, would be first on her agenda when she returned home. There could be no more procrastinating on this one. She made up her mind that it would be completed and sent before she went to bed that night.

The walk was what she needed to get back on track. Brandi met people she hadn't seen in a while and everyone wanted to visit, resulting in the outing extending a little longer than planned.

Finally at home with a cup of tea in hand, Brandi made her way to her office, where she plopped down on the lounge chair and pulled her notebook from the backpack. Time to review the report notes she had made during her lunch stop at The Bakery.

It wasn't long before the sun made its way into the western sky and through the window in her office. Normally, she didn't sleep during the day, but today, Brandi couldn't help but drop her head to the chair-back and close her eyes. The warm sun lulled her. Eyes heavy and body relaxed, she dozed.

When she woke, she was shivering. The sun had dropped out of sight, casting the room into early evening shadows. How long had she been sleeping? She peered at her wrist in the near darkness only to discover she wasn't wearing her watch.

She had been dreaming again. She felt certain that her being cold and shivering had more to do with the content of the dream than the sun going down.

Her tea was cold and her stomach was grumbling. She shivered again—a sign someone had walked over her grave, as her Gran used to say.

Standing, she wrapped the soft, comforting fibres of a blanket around her shoulders. A cup of something hot would do the trick to warm her up.

On her way to the kitchen, she decided to call Pete. Brandi reached for the phone and pressed the familiar keys of his number. The phone rang once. She hung up.

"This is silly," she said to herself. "I have nothing more to tell him, other than I think I've had another dream and I think it's related."

Brandi was still a little unnerved by the fact that there were two words written in her notebook. Worse yet, it didn't look like her handwriting. She stood staring out of the window contemplating her dream. The ringing of the telephone made her jump and brought her back to earth.

"Hello."

"I was going to hang up and come over if you didn't answer on that ring," said the gruff voice at the other end of the line. "Are you all right, Brandi?"

"I just woke up. It's nothing. I'm okay." Brandi tried to keep her voice calm and aloof.

"You phone me, let it ring once, and hang up. I call back and your phone rings nine times before you answer it."

Pete recognized the tone in her voice. He decided he would see for himself if things were as peachy as she was trying to pass off.

"I'm on my way over. Have you eaten?"

There was a pause in the conversation. Pete waited for her to answer.

"I didn't think so," he said impatiently. "Get ready. I'll be there to pick you up in half an hour."

The knock at the door told her Pete had arrived. He was the only person she was acquainted with that was averse to ringing the doorbell. His position on the matter was that doorbells were not dependable—his knuckles were.

She was doing up her coat when she opened the door to let him in. Eating out with Pete was predictable. They would drive to the little pizza place on the other side of the park or stop at The Bakery. It smelled like the latter had already won the coin toss.

Closing the door with his foot, he handed Brandi the bag from The Bakery.

"Hope you like Marnee's lasagna and garlic buns. Decided we should eat in. Just in case you still weren't feeling up to snuff."

"I told you, I'm fine."

Brandi took the bag and went into the kitchen. She was a little miffed with her friend for not believing there was nothing wrong. Placing the bag on the table, she turned to get the plates from the cupboard.

"Whatever you say, girl. Whatever you say."

She swung around and glared at the man she thought was her friend.

"Why don't you believe me?" she snapped.

Pete stood his ground and let her rant. When she took a breath, he stepped forward and put his hands on her shoulders.

"Because you know it's not true. I know you're letting these dreams consume you. The fact that you can't figure them out is eating away at you. You need to refocus on your life, Brandi. You need to start approaching this like it was one of your assignments. Like the professional I know you are, not some woman with half-baked ideas flapping off in whatever direction the wind blows!"

Brandi couldn't believe the angered tone that laced his words, but his harsh reproach hit home. Standing before him, she felt like a tremendous weight had lifted from her. Yet there was still the question of whether she would have to find the answers on her own. She'd thought Pete would help her, but now she wasn't so sure.

The awkward moment disappeared when Brandi moved away from Pete to finish setting the table. He busied himself taking the meal from the bag and filling the glasses with water.

Sitting across from each other, they talked about what had been going on in Notclin. Over the past few weeks, Brandi had spent little time on such matters. She was anxious and interested to hear what Pete had to say. He reached for more lasagna and continued the conversation.

"What have you been up to that you haven't a foggy clue one about the current events and gossip of our little town? Or need I ask?"

Brandi lay her fork down and took a drink of water. With the glass still in her hand, she started to talk.

"You're right. After our last meet up at The Bakery, I immersed myself in trying to figure out what these darned dreams mean. I've been through research boxes again and again. I've re-visited some of the sights I wrote about, but nothing came of it except worrying my editor, because I missed a team conference call."

Pete finished re-filling his plate and took another bun. "So the wear and tear on your vehicle and mostly your mind has you still grasping at straws?"

"Yes. Well, more or less. I guess you could say that."

"More or less? Come on, do you forget who you are having a conversation with?"

"I have more, but…" She trailed off.

"But what?"

"Let me finish before you turn your mind off."

Pete grinned at her and waved his hand for Brandi to continue while he carried on eating.

"You remember what I told you at The Bakery?"

He nodded.

"It's like I have some kind of imaginary spirit pushing me to go through the research boxes not once but four times."

Brandi held her hand in the air, showing four fingers sticking up.

"After the phone call from the magazine, there was something inside me that said enough already Westeron, get back to reality!"

Pete was thinking he couldn't agree more, but in view of their outburst before dinner, he thought it best to keep his words to himself. He didn't want to add any more fuel to the already smouldering fire.

"I decided to go for a walk to clear my mind. You know, go to the post office, pick up the mail, stop in to say hello to Marnee. Basically just get out of the house, and that's exactly what I did and it felt good. Eventually, I made it home to get started on my part of the team report."

Brandi stood to take her plate to the sink. She reached for the dish in front of Pete on her way by.

"Not done," he said, reaching again for the lasagna.

"Cheaper to pay for your room than your board." Brandi laughed, leaving the plate on the table in front of him.

"So you went for your walk, picked up the mail, saw Marnee, and came home? What were you doing between then and when you called me?"

"Made tea, went to the office, and like I said, started working on the team report."

"What's this team report you keep mentioning? Sounds pretty important."

Until the report was finished, and the draft had been distributed to the team members, she couldn't give out any of the details. Even after completion, only vague information could be discussed. On this, her contract with the magazine was very clear.

"Each of the magazine team members writes a report outlining the good and the bad of the past year. Once complete, we create what we call a future report. From this, the following eight months' worth of articles is decided upon. The report is distributed to the team to brainstorm. From that, preparations for the upcoming editions are compiled."

There, she thought, *I have told him what I can without giving specifics.*

Pete draped his arm over the back of the chair and watched Brandi as she moved around the kitchen.

"That's all you did this afternoon?"

"No, I fell asleep in the sun and had another dream."

His cough made her turn around.

"Was that why you called me and then hung up?"

"I wanted to share with you what I remembered about the dream."

"Why didn't you? Why haven't you?"

"After your pre-dinner lecture, I get the feeling you're not that interested in discussing the topic, so I decided not to bother."

The annoyance in his voice was evident when he answered.

"Let me make the decision of what I am and am not interested in. If I didn't give a damn, Brandi, you would be the first to know. I thought you at least knew that about me!"

She did know that. He had always been honest and straightforward.

"I only remember two words," she quietly answered.

"And they are?"

"Cold and pristine."

"Nothing more?"

"Nothing, unless you want to count flashbacks of the meadow, and I woke up shivering. Oh, and then there's the fact that those two words have been written in my notebook, but it doesn't look like my handwriting."

Pete stood to take his dishes to the sink at the other side of the room.

"Go gather up all your notes, please. Bring anything you can think of that might help us figure this thing out. I'll clear off the table and make us some tea. It's time we got down to some serious digging to get to the bottom of this."

"Probably going to need something stronger than tea to get through this," he mumbled, watching Brandi leave the room for her office.

Pete looked up from where he sat at the table to see Brandi coming from her office, her arms filled with papers and notebooks. He moved the mugs to one side in an effort to make the room they needed to spread everything out. He hoped Brandi had something in mind for their start point.

Pete's only thought was to review the maps. He was good with maps, and finding his way around the back roads was second nature to him.

"Let's mark all the places you went to on your homestead research and revisited over the last few weeks."

Spreading a marked-up map on the table, Brandi opened what she called her travel log.

Pete looked at the colour-coded grid lines before him. "Do you have a map that isn't all scarred up?"

Brandi produced a folded paper from the pile on the corner of the table.

"I'm way ahead of you," she replied, unfolding a new map.

"We can use the marked one and my notes to compare. Any I missed the second and third time around, the new map will catch as we check the locations off."

"I don't know why I'm getting involved with a clueless search for an unknown what or where," Pete mumbled.

"It isn't a clueless search!" Brandi retorted. "Remember, we also have what I remember from my dreams."

"That's just it, Brandi, they are dreams. You're chasing the clues from those dreams trying to figure them out."

She heard the sarcasm in Pete's voice but chose to ignore it, hoping the task before them would sway him.

After a few hours of cross-referencing, there was only one destination that had not been visited. The name appeared only once in the early part of the original information she had compiled for her homestead project. That page is where it had ended. There had been nothing further in her notes or the final work she had submitted to the magazine.

They sat staring at the pile of papers and open maps.

"Do you think this is another clue?" she asked. "Do you know anything about this place?"

"It's possible, but maybe it is what it is: just a place you decided not to include in your project."

Pete put his finger on the place where there was no mark identifying it as being visited. Brandi sat staring at the map. She couldn't remember anything about the location or why she hadn't included it. There was no recollection at all. It had taken this exercise of cross-referencing data to find it.

"I'd say it's about a three or four-hour drive from here, depending on the route you take. Sometimes more, when you consider that part of the country gets some good moisture, making the roads not so great to travel on."

The team project's deadline had to take precedence over anything to do with the dream research. Brandi required a foolproof plan, if she was going to do both. She still wasn't certain Pete was hooked on the idea of being further involved with the hunt for answers about her dreams, but now was the perfect time to brainstorm strategy. Maybe then she'd know if Pete Noll was on board.

"Would you like a beer?"

"Thought you'd never ask."

~3~

Brandi and Pete came to an agreement after they finished with the maps. She had convinced him to see what he could find out about the missed location on the map, and she would get her nose to the grindstone and prepare her report. It gave them breathing room from each other and a couple of weeks to complete their tasks. So there she sat, staring at blank paper, trying to initiate the first sentence of the first draft of the team report.

It should have been easy for Brandi to write. The good from her previous year's work was the Western Homesteads piece. The bad was not having long enough to work on the project. She felt there could have been more depth to the exposé, if she'd had more than a year to do the research and write it.

This was the basis for the proposal for future involvement with the magazine. She wanted to write more about homesteads in the West. She outlined the importance of becoming acquainted with the families, discovering the mystery of why they and their ancestors had settled there. The answers to most of the generic questions were the starting point to delving into the existence of the life she'd been exposed to while writing about homesteads.

Brandi already knew the editor loved her work, from his response to her Western Homesteads article. He had asked for more, and the team report was Brandi's opportunity to persuade the magazine to let her take the reader to the next level, using a personal approach. All she had, so far, was a list of words attempting to initiate sentences.

She sighed with relief when her brain kicked in with the first paragraph. The research would include local ranch or farm families with a history of homesteading in the area. The main criteria for a family to qualify would be a living relative still involved in some way with the running or managing of the business. This would coincide with localized venues, allowing her to showcase families with deep roots within the chosen territory.

The main obstacles would be convincing the short list of candidates to let her write about their family and the family's history. There was so much at stake on all fronts of the topic. It wouldn't be easy, but she'd have to find a way to make it happen.

The availability of history for future generations was something she'd become passionate about during the writing of Western Homesteads. Much of the old ways were being lost to modernization. This hard work that had once been a way of life was important, and too many people were clueless that it was now diminishing. She needed to tell their story. She needed to enrich those who were ignorant of the western way of life and impart to them the knowledge from those who grew up living the lifestyle.

Yawning, Brandi concluded that the outline for the team report would take more than this evening to complete. Her eyes were getting heavy when she finished the challenge of the point-form draft. Feeling good about her progress, she would now leave it alone for a few days before reviewing it. After that, the written draft would be formulated, readying it for the final edit and submission, within the time-frame she had been given.

Putting the work away, she turned off the light and headed to her bedroom with the dream research book tucked under her arm. Settled in bed, she opened the book, grinning at the pages of notes and plans already recorded. She found it akin to reading an outline for a piece of fiction.

She hoped to be able to find the clues to trigger where the dreams were coming from. She re-read the notes she'd made from recent trips. To get in touch with the surroundings, she would park on side roads to walk and feel the life that once was there, or lived there now. Nature, people, buildings, life, and history played a big part in her research.

Closing the book, she sat for a long time, letting the thoughts mesh and meld. Aware that she needed sleep, she hoped it would not elude her, as she turned out the light. Bathed in the glow of the moon through her window, she drifted off.

Brandi woke up exhausted from her subconscious night thoughts. She'd been walking in her dream. The familiar feeling of having company persisted. Neither frightened nor concerned about her feelings, she knew this dream had not been completed. Making some quick notes in her dream book, she got up to wander to the kitchen, deep in thought.

She had worked hard on her team report and now had a few days to do catch up around the house. The thought of going for a drive appealed to her. She'd call Pete to see if he'd like to go with her, though she doubted he would. It was a known fact around town that, when Pete Noll did things, he liked to get an early start. Looking at the clock on the wall, today's outing would definitely not be an early start. Thinking twice about inviting him along, she decided against it.

She was watching the day through the kitchen window, reflecting on her next move, when she was startled out of her daydream by the ringing of her phone.

"Hello."

"Hi. Brandi? Brandi Westeron?"

"Who is this?"

"I'm acquainted with Pete Noll."

Brandi's gut told her to move slowly with this caller.

"That's nice," Brandi answered with a little sarcasm in her voice. "What did you say your name was?"

After waiting for a response, Brandi was about to hang up when the female voice continued.

"I read your piece in the Homestead Life Quarterly magazine. I think you missed an opportunity by omitting one of the important homesteads in this part of the country."

Brandi was intrigued by what the woman said and decided it might be in her best interest to hear her out.

"Who is this?" Annoyance surfaced in Brandi's voice.

"I would like to meet with you, to talk about what I know."

For whatever reason, this woman did not want to divulge who she was and Brandi had had enough of the game.

"Well, thank you for calling. If you have read my article, you know that everything I do and write is transparent. I hide nothing. Until you want to give me your name, I see no reason to carry on this conversation with you, let alone meet with you! Goodbye."

Brandi ended the call, her mind racing. What did this woman want? How did she know Pete, or did she? Did she really have information she needed to know about? Was she some kind of kook? Who was she and how dare she use Pete's name? The biggest question was how she had gotten her telephone number. Pete would have told her if he had given her name to someone, and he would have given Brandi their name.

With the thoughts came trepidation. Had she just snubbed someone of importance? She looked at the phone and saw that the return number was unavailable. This added one more question. How could she get in touch with this person, if she decided to take the chance in finding out what the woman knew or wanted?

The phone rang again.

"I told you, if you are not going to tell me your name, I am not interested in speaking with you, on the phone or in person."

"Whoa! It's me."

"Pete! You are not going to believe what just happened."

Brandi launched into her rendition of the telephone conversation with a woman she didn't know. When she was finished and out of breath, all she heard was silence on the other end of the line.

"You there?"

"Ya, I'm here," he answered. "Do you want to go over that again, please? Only this time, try to talk a little slower so we can both digest what you're telling me."

Brandi repeated the story.

Pete stopped her in mid-sentence. "You've had another dream?"

"How did you know?"

"You just told me," he laughed.

"No! I was telling you about the crazy woman on the phone."

She hadn't realized that the first time around telling the story, she'd left out the part about her latest dream. Obviously, from Pete's comment, she had told him in the second version.

"That too," Pete replied. "I'd say the last twelve hours have been quite eventful for you. You got your team report started, slept, had a dream, a call from some unidentified person, and now you are talking to me. By the way, your phone number is listed in the 'Who's Who' of the town's directory. It's available to anyone who knows where you live, which is on your online bio."

Pete took a breath before continuing. "Your writing is catching the attention of the world outside your four walls. You might want to make some changes on your bio, if don't like strangers phoning you."

Brandi had never considered how public she was. She liked to write. She liked to share what she wrote. It never occurred to her that some crazy lady, or any other person, would try to get in touch with her because of it. Her fan mail, if you wanted to call it that, all went to the magazine before being handed over to her.

Pete was right; she would have to look into changing her social media and other personal information accessible to the public.

"Why did you call?" she asked, changing the subject and trying to calm her voice.

"Figured I'd touch base with you after our marathon to see if you had anything new come up."

"Well, I just brought you up to speed."

"Okay. It's pretty weird if you ask me. Give me a call if anything else surfaces over this."

"I will. You going to be around this week?"

"Nope, just getting ready to head out. I'll touch base with you when I get back."

Thinking this was the end of their conversation, Brandi was surprised when Pete carried on.

"This woman, the crazy one. You sure she didn't give you her name or some clue as to who she is?"

"No, she didn't. Why? Is something not holding true or did she say something you might have recognized?"

"Can't see why anyone would use my name. You're sure she said Pete Noll, not P.C. Noll, like it was in your magazine article?"

"Like I said. She told me, "I'm acquainted with Pete Noll." That tells me she either knows you personally or knows of you somehow."

"Okay then. I guess you'll just have to meet with her and find out who she is for both of us."

"That's only going to happen if she calls back. I didn't get her name and her number didn't show up on the call display."

"You'll figure it out; you always do. Talk to you when I get back."

Waking with a jolt had become a normal occurrence for Brandi Westeron. Not quite sure what it was that woke her this time, she lay in bed, looking at the grey dawn out the bedroom window, and trying to resurrect the details of last night's dream experience. She thought that, if she could just lay there, maybe she would remember more.

Trying to make sense out of recent oddities in her life, combined with the dreams, was starting to take a toll on her thoughts and sleep process.

She had taken notes about the dreams after the first one a few months before. The notes seemed to help her with the feelings and the search for answers. Although there had been no blazing light or Aha moment, writing was her way of making sense of something she could not remember enough of. It was an attempt to put her mind at rest and pinpoint the pieces of her REM sleep state that eluded her in the search for the missing pieces of the puzzle.

Reaching for her notebook and pencil, Brandi started to jot down her first waking thoughts. Doves. Hollyhocks. Axe. Not much to go on, but that was all she could remember.

She pushed the covers back and stretched. Leaving the warmth of her bed, she stopped to wash her face and slip into her robe. The automatic start on the coffee maker had kicked in and the welcoming aroma of brewing coffee met her halfway down the hall. Notebook in hand, it was time to seriously review all of her dream clues.

Drinking her coffee, she scanned the notes she'd made, trying without success to put some semblance of order to them. There had been four dreams so far and last night numbered five. Each had been different, but all left her with an urge to pursue the clues. She didn't know if it was the writer in her, curiosity, or just plain stubborn orneriness directing her to not give up. Now that her team report had been submitted, she would have more time to focus on this dream research.

It was Saturday, and that meant Marnee would be featuring the breakfast special at The Bakery. She'd stayed indoors for the past week, meeting all of her deadlines, and grinned at the thought of going for a bite. With any luck at all Pete would be there having coffee before he left town, and she could share last night's dream words with him.

Entering The Bakery, Brandi was surprised there was no one in the shop she recognized. In the corner where Pete usually sat was a woman with her head down, writing between mouthfuls of food. At the table by the door sat a young couple enjoying the $6.99 Saturday special. Brandi walked to the counter where the coffee pot sat. She filled a cup and called hello to Marnee.

"Breakfast special or just coffee?" was the reply from the doorway to the kitchen.

"Special, half order, please."

Her friend gave the thumbs up and turned to go back into the kitchen.

"You seen Pete this morning?"

"Haven't seen him for about a week," Marnee called over her shoulder.

Brandi picked up her coffee and walked towards a table by the window. The woman in the corner had looked up and was watching her make her way across the room.

"Won't you join me, Ms. Westeron?"

Brandi froze. The hair on her neck stood up and goosebumps formed on her arms. The voice was unmistakably the unidentified caller from last week. The woman smiled, gesturing for Brandi to join her.

Brandi's gut still told her this woman was not who she seemed.

"Joining you will depend entirely on whether you are going to provide your name and why you are here. I told you on the phone that I am not interested in speaking with anyone not willing to identify themselves."

"And I told you, I am acquainted with Pete Noll."

"Well he's not here to vouch for you, so no thank you, I'll sit by myself."

The woman stood, and making her way over to Brandi, she extended her hand to shake.

"My name is Jessi Smalts. I think you'll want to hear what I have to say about the once prominent Cedor Ranch. You may have heard of it?"

The short, red-haired woman motioned towards the chair again.

"As for Mr. Noll, I said I was acquainted with him. That doesn't mean I know him personally."

The ranch's name rang true with Brandi. It had been the one on her list she'd not included in the article—the only one that had not been marked when she and Pete had done the cross-referencing exercise. The lady had Brandi's attention. She wished Pete were here to listen.

Brandi was still in a state of shock after her impromptu meeting with Jessi Smalts. The breakfast Marnee had set before her remained uneaten while she took notes and asked questions of this woman she had just met. She couldn't understand how she had missed including the Cedor Ranch in her article.

The information overload Jessi had provided was something Brandi would eventually have to confirm. The bits of Cedor Ranch history seemed plausible, and she was certain Pete could help her in that regard, but there was always the no-darn-way factor when you hear something for the first time and can't believe what you're hearing.

When the two women parted, Jessi promised to keep in touch, if there was any more information to share. In parting, she asked Brandi to keep the Cedor Ranch on her radar. Jessi had given Brandi some specific dates to look into, and suggested she talk further with Pete about the ranch and its history. Brandi wanted to know more, but Jessi declined, saying it was not her place to do so and that she had already divulged more than she should have. The meeting only led to more questions.

Leaving The Bakery, Brandi's mind was in a quandary over the enticing tidbits Jessi Smalts had shared with her. She'd promised herself to focus on the dream clues and to let everything else fall into place when and if it should.

"Maybe with a bit of planning, I could include a visit to the Cedor Ranch to find out for myself what the mystery is all about," she murmured.

Meeting the Smalts woman introduced an additional twist to her planned research. She now considered the possibility of extending her fact-finding efforts farther afield.

Brandi was thankful her career allowed flexibility to work wherever she wanted. The dreams and Jessi's information warranted the need to explore beyond the walls of her home and travel comfort zone. In past outings, discoveries of meadows and cold, pristine creeks were frequent, yet none possessed the feeling of being drawn to them, like the magnet that surrounded the words in her dreams.

A normal research routine included driving until noon, a stop at a local cafe for lunch, and then head back home by a different route. This was the first time she'd had the urge to go beyond those boundaries in a long time. Determined to find lodging in the general direction she planned to explore, Brandi went in search of a bed and breakfast she could use as a home base.

Several attempts to reach Pete since Saturday's meeting with Jessi had failed. He would continue to be on her radar as she travelled. She needed him to enlighten her on what he knew about the Cedor Ranch's history.

By early afternoon, her overnight bag was packed and sat waiting for her by the door. Laptop and camera gear rested beside the bag, along with a fresh thermos of coffee for the drive. Brandi had told the B & B that her arrival would be around 5:30, giving herself ample time to stop along the way, if she found something of interest to make notes about or photograph.

The lady Brandi spoke to at the B & B invited her to join them for the evening meal. Brandi explained she was coming to do some research and would be using their home for her base. The lady had suggested they could provide bag lunches for her to take on her daily outings. The extra cost had been minimal and Brandi had agreed, because the idea of not having to find a place to eat while she drove around the country suited her just fine.

Behind the wheel of her truck, Brandi decided to take one of the alternate routes to her destination, which would include gravel roads and less traffic. The solitude would give her time to think and update her plan of attack on this project. She turned off the main road and headed west. The feeling that she was not alone on the journey was oddly comforting, and made her smile.

Cattle guards and gravel roads were common in Brandi's line of work. Her route to Saddle Ridge B & B took her through country she'd travelled often. It was turning out to be a pleasant and uneventful drive, and she was looking forward to reaching her destination and settling in.

The large gate loomed ahead. This was the final turn, according to the GPS coordinates she had keyed in before leaving home. The sight of a log home, with a few outbuildings across the creek, greeted her when she pulled into the yard. *Perfect location,* she thought, gathering her belongings from the seat beside her.

The door opened before she reached the steps, and a tall, middle-aged couple came out to welcome her.

"You must be Brandi. I'm Eileen Smythen. Please call me Eileen. This is my husband, Gordon. Best call him Gord, if you want to get him to answer." She laughed.

Brandi set down her luggage to shake their hands. Gord picked up her bags, leading the way into the large mudroom.

"Your room is downstairs. I hope that will be all right for you."

"That'll be fine. Is there a WiFi connection? I never thought to ask when I made the reservation. I noticed my cell service was sporadic coming in from the highway, too."

"It depends on the weather. We're surrounded by enough mountains and hills that modern technology takes a back seat to the clouds, fog, wind, rain, and snow," Gord said, starting down the steps. "That's the best we can offer."

Brandi was not phased by the lack of the technology she took for granted at home. This would give her time to write without distractions and concentrate on finding some answers to her dreams.

Gord opened the door to the room, placing the bags inside on the floor.

"Make yourself at home. Dinner and breakfast are served in the dining area off the kitchen, back up the stairs to your right. Dinner will be ready at 6:00. If there is anything you need in the meantime, come up and let us know."

Digging through her backpack for a notebook and pencil, she contemplated how much time she would have before dinner. There was time to sit on the bench beside the window and jot down questions she wanted to ask her hosts. They might have some of the preliminary answers to get her off on the right foot and get a feel for the direction she would be headed in the morning.

In the outside pocket of the backpack, she found the map with the B & B already marked. Ten-mile-radius circles were drawn around her home for the next week. Unless the Smythens told her otherwise, she was going to start from the farthest circle and travel as many of the gravel roads as possible, hoping the answers would be out there somewhere.

Glancing at her watch, it was 5:55 and time to get the show on the road. Brandi picked up her notebook and map before making her way back upstairs to have dinner with Eileen and Gord Smythen.

"Hi. Am I too early?"

"Not at all," Eileen assured her. "It'll be about ten minutes or so. Gord had to go check on a sick cow and will be back any minute. Would you care for a beverage while we wait?"

"I can wait until dinner, thanks," replied Brandi, leaning on a chair. "On second thought, I would love a glass of cold water."

Eileen retrieved a glass from the sideboard, filling it with ice water.

"It's interesting that you have a bed and breakfast and run a ranch too."

"Diversity in this modern world is what allows a lot of the rural folks to hold onto their heritage. Not just the traditional way of life they grew up with, but land that's been in families for generations."

Brandi's interest was immediately piqued. Not wanting to give away any of her future writing plans, she shelved the urge to start asking questions about their family's heritage until Gord returned. The thought of this couple possibly being candidates for the next exposé made Brandi giddy inside. Later would be soon enough to ask a few initial questions. For now, she would make small talk with Eileen Smythen.

Gord stood at the head of the table, hands resting on the back of the chair.

"So you want to know all about us? I thought you said you were here doing some sort of personal search."

"No. I mean yes. Well, sort of," Brandi stammered, a bit flustered. "I am here doing research on a personal topic. That is true, but I find your situation here very interesting. I would be lying if I said I didn't want to know more."

Gord sat down and looked at Brandi at the other side of the table.

"Well, I guess we could discuss that with you at some time, or is that what you are planning to do this evening?" He pointed to her notebook and map, which she'd left on the counter.

Brandi was embarrassed. She did not want to offend these people, but she didn't want to lose the opportunity to do a story on them either. The notebook and map had come to her rescue.

"What kind of information are you looking for?" asked Gord.

"I was hoping you could give me some information on some of the places I should include in my travels."

Brandi was glad to have the topic changed. While Eileen finished bringing the dinner to the table, she talked about her research, leaving out the part that all the clues were based on dreams.

After dinner, conversation was a mixture of travel, cattle, and writing. The three of them had looked at the maps and discussed what she hoped to accomplish while she was staying with them.

"Time to call it a night," announced Gord, after seeing Brandi hide a yawn behind her hand.

Standing and stretching, Brandi nodded in agreement. Eileen had already told her breakfast would be served at 7:00. The morning meal would be the perfect time to discuss the additional notes she planned to make back in her room, and to hear what Gord had to say about the short-cut directions that would reduce her road time.

~5~

"Good morning, did you sleep well?" Eileen asked, pouring Brandi a mug of coffee.

Brandi laughed. "Like a baby. I thought, with it being so quiet, I wouldn't be able to go to sleep. Didn't take me long."

"Gord's just in from doing chores. We'll eat as soon as he's done washing up."

"Did I hear someone say my name?" the tall, grey-haired man asked, coming into the room. "'Morning, Brandi. Did you have a good sleep?"

"Good morning, and yes, one of the best in a long time. Thanks."

They had a leisurely morning meal while visiting about Brandi's research and her Western Homesteads article. Both Eileen and Gord had read the piece and were impressed to have its author staying with them, although they did not say so aloud.

When the dishes were cleared away, Gord invited Brandi to spread out her map and bring her notebook, so she could jot down the shortcut information. He started by telling her that most of the range roads and township roads would eventually intersect with a secondary or main highway. Brandi nodded, confirming that she already knew these roads were a combination of pavement and gravel. They reviewed the routes she'd considered taking, discussing the benefits of each and making some changes.

Gord explained that she should start in the outside circle, adding that, if she were to cover even half the areas, she would need to be on the road by seven every morning. He recommended that, for today, he and his wife would tour her around to some of the neighbours. Their introduction would open gates, literally, to private land closed to the public.

Brandi was thrilled with the thought of being in a vehicle for most of the day with the Smythens. She was certain they were walking books of knowledge on the area and its history. She'd garner information from them, while she gathered data for her dream research.

"While you get ready, and Eileen makes some lunch to take along, I'll make some calls to see if anyone's moving cattle. You might get some good pictures if that's something you're interested in."

Back in her room, Brandi deposited her coat and camera bag by the door before packing an extra pair of socks, the maps, notebook, and an extra pen and pencil in her backpack. Happy that she had all she would need for the outing, she picked up her belongings and grabbed an apple from the welcome basket on the dresser on the way out of the room.

The Smythens were waiting for her in the mudroom. A cooler with their lunches and cold beverages was in Gord's hands and Eileen had a thermos in each of hers.

"We don't take coffee with us," Eileen said, raising one of the thermoses to make a point. "We take hot water and make tea as we want it. That way if the water cools off, we have extra drinking water, other than what is in the cooler. If you'd like to take coffee along, I can fill a couple of go-cups for you."

Eager to get going, Brandi declined the coffee, opening the door for her hosts.

"We'll take our truck this morning," Gord said. "I need to pick some stuff up in town."

Brandi hid her displeasure from her hosts, as she continued on to her own vehicle. She liked to be the driver. She saw things she didn't when she was the passenger. She knew this couple was going out of their way for her though, and she was appreciative. *Travelling with the Smythens might just make being a passenger fun,* she thought.

"I just need to get my mud boots."

Gord continued as if Brandi hadn't said a word.

"We'll go south on the highway, then head east on the Sky Hills Road. That will take us to some of the places we marked on your map within the circles."

Brandi giggled as she climbed into the back seat of the crew cab. This was going to be a good day. She took her map and notebook from her backpack and settled into the back seat of the truck.

The first stop was to have coffee with a neighbour, about eight miles away from the Smythens. When the trio was leaving, the Longs invited Brandi to return later in the week to explore their homestead ranch. She was looking forward to the return visit, and by then she would have had time to talk with Gord and Eileen about the family living there.

After enjoying the hospitality of their neighbours, the threesome carried on their way. They chatted about their coffee stop, and the Smythens provided her with quite a bit of helpful information about the Longs. It didn't take long for her to fill up a few pages with point-form notes.

Gathering leads and details for her future stories was stonewalling her dream research. *Focus,* she thought. *I need to focus, if I am going to get any answers about these dreams.*

The trail to the old Shire place was located just past the halfway point to town. This is where the Smythens decided would be a good place to have lunch. Gord pulled off the gravel road, stopping the truck halfway up a grassy knoll. When Brandi looked out her window, she sucked in her breath.

"Holy..." she whispered to herself. The view was something she had never seen before and only imagined existed.

She took her camera to the top of the little hill and started taking pictures in every direction. Some of the views were blocked by trees and others were wide open and spectacular.

"This is the reason I carry extra camera batteries," she said to no one in particular.

Eileen had set the food out on the tailgate, and she was pouring hot water into cups.

"Get some good shots?" Gord asked, when she set her camera in the box of the truck and reached for some water.

"I can't believe I have never been up here before. There is some amazing scenery in this part of the world. I'm looking forward to seeing the results on my computer screen when we get home tonight."

She pointed to the blaze marks in the two trees nearby. "What are those for?"

"That marks the trail-head to the old Shire place. They're found along the trail most of the way in. It takes about half an hour to get there, if you've never been or you don't know what you are looking for." Gord took a bite of his sandwich and a drink of tea. "We have time today to walk into the building site, if you'd like."

"Like! I would love to!" Brandi couldn't contain her excitement. "Who owns the place? Is there any family living that I could talk to? Are the buildings usable? Does anyone live there now?"

The questions came in a rush and when she stopped to take a breath, Gord interrupted.

"Don't know. Don't know. Some. Don't think so." He laughed at the puzzled look on Brandi's face.

"I just answered all your questions. Isn't that what you want? For us to answer your questions?"

"Gord," his wife said sternly. "Quit teasing the girl."

"I deserved that." Brandi giggled. "Now, let me think about what Gord said and see if I can pair it up with my questions."

"We had best get going. We'll answer your questions the best we can while we're walking. It's a pretty easy trek." Gord took his rifle from the scabbard behind the back seat.

"Will we need that?" Brandi asked.

"I hope not. Best to be safe than sorry when you're in bear country."

With the cooler packed away in the cab, the three started along the marked path towards the old homestead.

Brandi was mesmerized with finding the blaze marks on the trees along the trail. Some had been freshened but most were dark scars made long ago with knives or other tools.

"Why are some of them up so high?" asked Brandi, pointing over their heads. "You can hardly see them."

Gord explained the marks were most likely some of the first made along the trail. Over time, the trees grew and new trail markers would have been made lower down on the trunks. He pointed to a tree with both old scabbed-over marks and one lower down starting to blacken.

"Like these."

Brandi stopped to take pictures, thinking she would have to make notes when they reached their destination. She chastised herself for not bringing her tape recorder.

"Is Shire the name of the people who proved up this land for their homestead?" Brandi asked.

"No, that's not it, but I can't recall their name. Do you, Eileen?"

"It was an odd name, if I remember right. It will be in the area history book that we have at home. I think it will tell you that no one could pronounce it properly, so they called it the Shire place. That's how a lot of places got their names back then. Come to think of it, it's still how we name things." Eileen laughed.

"They owned Shire horses. One of the first places in this area to have them. They used them for everything. Farming, hitched to the wagon to go to town, and every so often you would see one of the boys riding one like a saddle horse."

They reached a large clearing in the trees that revealed some corrals and old buildings.

"The corrals are kept up and used as holding pens when local ranchers are gathering cattle in the fall. We all take a turn doing the maintenance. The cabin is waterproof. It'll do in a pinch for a line shack, if you're stuck out here overnight or a storm blows in. The barn's seen better days, but the far end has a couple of usable horse stalls. The roof is still in pretty good shape considering its age. These buildings were built using some real fine craftsmanship."

Continuing to take pictures, Brandi listened to Gord. She zoomed in on the barn and then let the camera drop to her side.

"Oh!" she whispered, starting towards the barn before swerving towards the house.

"You okay, Brandi? You look like you've seen a ghost."

"In my previous research on homesteads, correct me if I'm wrong, I learned 'dovetail' is the term used for how the logs were hewn to join at the corners. To look like a dove's tail."

Eileen caught up with Brandi at the edge of the house. "Are you okay?" she asked again.

"This is one of the clues I was taking about last night. Dovetail. I don't know what it means yet, but I'm going to find out."

Brandi slowly walked around the house, taking in all the details. "Did they have any kind of a garden here?"

"There's a rose bush by the back door, but I think the deer ate most of it. Every few years you'll see a couple of spindly flowers. There's a rhubarb patch over near the barn. Other than that, nothing else still grows here that I know of. Any garden that you can recollect, Gord?"

Brandi's mind was whirling. Dovetails, but no axe, no meadow, no hollyhocks, and no pristine cold anything. She pulled her notebook out of her backpack and found a place to sit on the woodpile next to the Smythens.

"Do you know who owns this property now?"

"Heard some company bought this and a few other prime abandoned locations in the area. We expected things to happen. To change. You know, new people and their wild ideas to build dude ranches, retreats, and the like," said Gord. "But so far, the properties have been left as they are, other than what the locals do. Every so often, something will get fixed and none of us know who or how it was done. Like the place has a guardian or spirit keeper."

Brandi knew exactly what Gord was talking about. How many times in the past few months did things just happen?

"Is there a land registry office in town?"

"Yes, but they may not be open by the time we get there."

"Dang!" she muttered.

Oh well, she would have cell service in town and could call Pete to get him to check this out. Squirrelling out information about places is what he'd excelled at on the last article he had helped her with. After all, he had told her to face her dream research like a writing assignment: dig, gather, write.

The rest of the trip to town, Brandi made notes in between re-reading back pages and gazing out the window at the passing scenery. If she could find out who owned the old Shire place, it might have a chance of inclusion in her next project. Then, all she needed to do was locate a living relative to make it happen.

Laying her head back against the seat, she closed her eyes. Her thoughts turned to the dovetails and her dreams. Soon the movement of the truck and the sun on her face lulled her to sleep, until the sound of Gord's voice announcing they had arrived in town woke her.

It was late in the afternoon by the time they returned from the outing. The aroma of a hearty meal of beef stew simmering in the crockpot welcomed them. Eileen had prepared a salad and garlic bread before they had left, and the three of them visited while the table was being set and the bread was warming.

Brandi excused herself as soon as she was finished dinner. She wanted to review the pictures she had taken, go over her notes, and add more information from conversations of the day.

Disappointed not to reach Pete while they were in town, she'd left a message for him to do some checking into the Shire place if he had time. Her check-in call to Marnee had been a little more successful. The Bakery owner assured her all was well in Notclin, and she had seen Pete the day before at the post office, so he was around.

"You know Pete," she'd said. "He's always busy doing something." Marnee promised to remind him to check the messages on his phone if she saw him.

Settled on the big couch in the downstairs common room, Brandi started downloading the pictures taken earlier in the day. While the download was completing on its own, she spread the map out on the coffee table. Opening her notebook, she started the review of the day. That was the last she remembered before falling asleep.

Far away, voices spoke quietly. "Let her sleep," they said. "She's had a full day." Brandi couldn't get her mind to clear the fog away. She was exhausted, yet knew she needed to wake up. Deep inside her thoughts, she struggled to reach consciousness.

Groggy but finally awake, Brandi willed her body to get off the couch and move around. She really needed to go through everything while it was fresh in her mind. She went to the bottom of the stairs, listening for any noises to indicate her hosts were still up. There was a light on in the mudroom, and there were low murmurs coming from the kitchen.

"Hello?" she called, reaching the top of the stairs.

"Did you have a nice nap? We were just going to have some tea and dessert. Would you like to join us?" Eileen offered.

"That would be nice. How long did I sleep? What time is it?"

Brandi made her way to the table, where Gord was enjoying a piece of pie.

"It's almost 9:00. Not sure how long you slept. Did you get any of your work done?" he asked between bites.

"The pictures are downloaded. The map is spread out on the table, and that, I'm afraid, is as much as I accomplished."

They sat at the table and talked about the day. The registry office had been closed when Eileen and Brandi had walked there, leaving Gord to look after his town chores. The ladies had stopped for a quick look in a few of the shops, and Brandi had picked up a local real-estate news in the off chance there was a listing that might catch her eye for future research.

It was almost eleven when Brandi said her goodnights. Her mind was in chaos with all the information piling up. The decision to make the next day an under-the-radar day, staying close to home base, was not hard to make.

Tonight she would finish the evening looking through the book of local history Eileen had retrieved from their library, reading up on the names of the owners of the old Shire place and any others the Smythens had mentioned. Tomorrow morning, she would tackle everything she'd recorded today.

~6~

Meeting people, hearing new stories, and finding the dovetails—yesterday had been exhilarating and exhausting. She had finished it off by reading the history book into the wee hours of the morning. Confirming the story Gord and Eileen had told her about the old Shire place and the then-owner's last name, which she also couldn't pronounce, was all included in her notes to share with Pete.

With a few hours of sleep behind her, Brandi sat enjoying a cup of coffee, reading the real-estate news she'd picked up in town. The paper was much like the one available in the small town she lived in. It was filled with real-estate listings, tips on repairs, and curb-appeal pointers. Halfway through the paper, an article caught her eye under the heading 'Home on the Range'. The contributor had written about how plants, shrubs, and trees around a homestead could tell a lot about the people who had broke ground there.

Sparse amounts of perennial flowers usually indicated the lack of female presence; however, in this man's world, it was normal to find a rhubarb plant or two around the property. Common plants included those producing good seed heads and root systems. Each could be harvested for future planting and trading. The want for a bit of civilization in a sometimes harsh land would have the lady of the house nurturing pansies, hollyhocks, lavender, and other herbs, alongside a prolific vegetable garden.

The author then went on to list several places known for their beautiful heritage gardens. Some, she offered, had been abandoned or were overgrown and running amuck from self-seeding. Others were groomed and well-mannered around homes still in use. The write-up finished by providing a list of historical and botanical groups found around the area.

Brandi couldn't believe her luck in locating so much information in a half-page article. She made some notes with the thought of using the contact information to reach out to the writer.

Voices and laughter coming from up the stairs told her the Smythens were in the kitchen. Folding the paper open to the piece she'd read, she tucked it under her arm to take upstairs. She was certain her hosts would know if any of the gardens the woman had described were within the research circles on her map.

The thought of killing two birds with one stone made her smile. Hollyhocks had been prevalent in her fifth dream, and she could only hope to find some to welcome her like the dovetailed logs had. Being able to locate additional homesteads, meeting the criteria for her next series of articles, would be a bonus.

This is already starting to be a good day, she thought. It was time to join her hosts for breakfast and continue with her quest for answers.

Brandi had been at the B & B for two nights, and it already felt like this place, and the people who owned it, had been a part of her life for a long time. They talked at length about the article in the paper. The lady who had written it was a retired school teacher who was always digging up tidbits of information, Eileen told them.

From the list in the paper, the Smythens confirmed that a few of the places were within Brandi's research circles. Gord offered to sit with her later, to find the sites on the map and give her some directions on how to get to them. In the meantime, he had some fence repairs to do and excused himself to get on with his chores.

Eileen was busy clearing up the remnants of breakfast. For her, it would soon be time to start preparations for the evening meal. Tonight, there were additional guests arriving in time for dinner, and she apologized to Brandi for not being able to spend much time with her.

"No worries. You and Gord have been a great information bank already. Is there anything I can help you with, besides staying out of your hair?"

"Thanks for asking, but I have everything under control. You go and do whatever you need to."

Brandi was eager to look at the pictures from the outing. She had hoped the Smythens would be able to sit in on the screening, so she could ask questions that might come up. As it was, she would have to take notes and ask later.

Brandi set off down the stairs, with a carafe of coffee and a plate of snacks Eileen had given her. "Just in case you need a brain pick me up," she'd said.

Downstairs, Brandi retrieved her research material from her room. She had long since set up a system to organize where and when she had taken pictures. Her writing demanded easy access to the photographs when she needed them.

She curled up on the couch with her notebook open to the first pages of yesterday's drive. In the left margin, she had written:

- Pictures 1 - 36 B & B/Sky Hill Road
- Pictures 37 - 90 Lunch Break
- Pictures 91 - 127 Trail to Shire Place
- Pictures 128 - 311 Shire Place
- Pictures 312 - 563 Return Trail Head/Town/Return to B & B

There were almost six hundred pictures to review, make comments on, and further catalogue. She was happy she'd made the decision to stay at the B & B today. It was going to give her time to go through each section and choose a minimal number of pictures to show Gord when he got home.

Just before noon, Brandi took her first break to do more than refill her coffee and get another snack. She needed some fresh air and went in search of Eileen, to find out where she could and couldn't go on the ranch. With a few suggested places that were secluded, yet close by, Brandi strolled along the road, making her way towards the bridge.

Taking her time, enjoying the fresh air and quiet, she thought about the short list of pictures she'd chosen to talk to Gord about. Some were of scenery, some intricate details, and a few were "oh wow" moments. Whatever the reason for choosing them, she had been drawn to each without question.

Lowering herself onto a rock near the creek, Brandi turned her face to the sun and closed her eyes. The gentle breeze and talking creek were the only sounds.

Slowly her jumbled thoughts were plucked from her mind, leaving a clear view of her dream clues. The feeling that she wasn't alone was strong enough to make her open her eyes, anticipating someone or something would be there.

"I'm being silly," she whispered under her breath, standing to look around. "Time to get back to work."

Retracing her steps back to the house, she was almost at her destination when Gord pulled up beside her in the truck.

"Give you a lift?"

"No thanks, I'll meet you at the house."

Gord nodded and left her to walk the rest of the way. He knew what this place could do to people, and the look on Brandi's face told him she had made the connection.

The Smythens were visiting in the mudroom when Brandi came into the house.

"Have a good walk?" Eileen asked.

"The best!"

"Whenever you're ready to go over pictures, let me know," Gord offered. "Eileen has made a cold lunch, if you're interested in working while we eat."

"That's a great idea. I'll go get my laptop and notes."

"Why don't you two have a look at them downstairs? Gord can bring the tray with the lunch after he washes up." Eileen waved towards the dining room. "I would love to have you up here, but I'll want to be looking over your shoulders, and I know I won't get a thing done. I think downstairs would be best." She laughed.

Brandi had set up a folder called "Shire Short List" to store the pictures to show Gord. There were still about fifty pictures she needed to go through from the last leg of the outing, but they would have to wait for another time.

She heard Gord coming down the stairs whistling. Setting the tray on the table next to the computer, he sat down beside Brandi, took a sandwich, and pointed to the laptop. "Where do you want to begin?"

Brandi felt she needed to explain her picture files and how they worked with her margin notes. Gord nodded.

"I have picked no more than five pictures from each file to go into the short list. If you want to look at others when we're done here, I would gladly share them. There are still some left from the trip from town back to here that I haven't got to yet. We might want to have a quick look at those after we look at the chosen ones."

"Okay, let's do this."

"The first few are from your neighbour's place. I'd like to skip those for now and maybe revisit them before I go back to their place later this week."

Gord was finishing his sandwich and gave her a thumbs up.

The next batch was from their lunch stop on Sky Hills Road. Gord remembered Brandi taking several pictures from the top of the knoll, and wondered if she had included any of those in her final cut. He soon got his answer when the first one flashed up on the screen.

"Nice," he said, before he took a drink of his coffee. "Good clear shot of the mountains."

"The mountains are the icing in the picture. I was focusing on what looked like the tip of a field showing at the end of this stand of trees." Brandi pointed. "Here," she said, tapping the screen. "Can you tell me anything about the field?"

Gord shifted so he could get a better look at the screen.

"That stand of trees is the property line for our neighbours where we stopped." He leaned back on the couch. "The field was once a wild hay meadow. Hasn't been hayed for years. It's used mainly for a holding meadow when cattle are moved through there. There's a line shack and some corrals at the other end, behind the trees over there." He pointed to the edge of the picture. "I'll call over to the Longs and confirm they still have access from their place. If they do, you could include it when you go there to visit."

We've just looked at one picture, and there's more questions than answers, she thought, as she continued to fill the page with notes.

"Next is on our way to the old Shire place."

Gord was about to speak when Brandi put her hand up to stop him.

"Just so you know, I understand about the blaze marks on a trail, and why they are made, but why would these ones be off course and have such scraggly edges?"

Leaning closer to the screen, Gord let out a slow breath. "Good eye! Those, young lady, are not human trail markers. Those are made by a bear."

"Bear scratch, right?" Brandi asked.

"You have done your homework, I see," he replied with a nod.

"Some," she said. "Were they made this year?"

"I would say early this spring, by how raw they look. They do that to mark their territory, letting other bears in the area know they are there. It's like a calling card saying, 'I'm this big, and I was here first'."

Brandi was again scribbling in her notebook.

Gord continued. "It's a good idea to be aware of your surroundings and animal sign when you're out there. Seeing marks like this confirms you are in bear country."

"Thanks for confirming the bear info."

"Is this part of your dream project?"

"No, I just wanted to be sure my notes are correct and in line with how I was thinking."

Gord reached for another sandwich.

"You'd best eat something, if you don't want Eileen giving you what for."

They flipped through a few more pictures while they finished eating. Brandi asked easy questions that just confirmed facts. When they reached the photos that had been taken at the old Shire place, Brandi's line of questioning got technical and personal, based on what she had read in the local history book Eileen had loaned her.

"I couldn't find in the book whether they would've prepared all the logs themselves with the dovetail ends, or if they'd been done by some other local."

"They did all their own work, or so the stories say. Most of the old timers around here would have been pretty young back then, to have any stories that they would personally remember, but some have diaries their folks kept, and this is how the tales get passed along. There's no disputing the fact they were good carpenters. Artisans would be a better way to describe them. Their work can be seen at several of the old abandoned places and on some of the ranches nearby. They would trade work for preserves, chickens, baking, quilts, and supplies. Things they would have had if there'd been women-folk living on the place."

Brandi made a note in the corner of her book to try to reach Pete the next time she had some cell service. Maybe he had come up with something about the Shire homestead since the last voicemail she'd left him.

"I am going to try and get back to town and visit the registry office before I go home. Sure would like to know who that place is owned by now."

"You have a lot of things you want to take care of before you leave us, young lady. You might have to come back and visit again, if you don't get it all done. And now I have some chores that need looking after, so we'll have to continue this later."

The Shire pictures out of the way, Brandi was happy to have some quiet time to herself. She was now faced with the decision of reading over what she had written during her time with Gord, going through the Lang pictures, or sorting the last batch of downloaded photos. Looking at her watch, there was time enough to sort the last of the pictures before the other guests arrived and dinner was served.

~7~

The new guests were repeat visitors at Saddle Ridge. It wasn't long before everyone was visiting and bantering back and forth. When Eileen served the after-dinner refreshments, Brandi took leave of the conversation and gaiety.

Returning to her room determined to finish with the last bunch of pictures, she noticed it was later than she thought. She completed her task of sorting through the balance of the pictures taken on their way home from town. Disappointed none had grabbed her attention on the first pass through, the late hour dictated she leave well enough alone if she was going to get any sleep before heading out in the morning.

She'd made arrangements with Eileen to have muffins and fruit to take with her, so she could be on her way early. Gord promised to have her thermos filled with coffee. The planned day away would take her to the outside circle on her map, and hopefully give her some insight to her dreams, rather than more questions.

Brandi lay in the darkness of her room, thinking about the last two days. She was certain that the dovetail finish on the logs at the old Shire place was telling her something. The article about homesteads with hollyhocks had given her more to ponder, and then there was the feeling of not being alone at the creek. She was sure these were all bits of the puzzle yet to be fitted together. Listening to the coyotes yipping at the moon from across the creek, she drifted off to sleep.

It was still dark when Brandi left her room to start the day of exploring. The smell of coffee met her at the bottom of the stairs.

"Thank you, Gord," she whispered into the dimly lit stairwell.

In the kitchen, she found a note from Eileen explaining what was in her snack pack and wishing her a fruitful day. Beside it stood her coffee-filled thermos and some water.

Letting herself out of the house, she could see the sun trying to make its way over the ridge.

"It's going to be a spectacular sunrise," she murmured to herself.

"Better get the camera ready," said a deep voice from beside the house.

Brandi jumped and swung around.

"Gord?"

"Expecting someone else?" he chuckled.

"Thought you'd be gone to do chores."

"Just getting to it. Figured I might tell you of a place of interest that came to mind."

Brandi was struggling to get her backpack and camera into her truck and get her notebook out at the same time. Finally in her grasp, she lifted her foot to rest it on the floor of the truck, so she could use her knee for a table.

"Shoot," she said, pen poised and ready.

"If you want to change your plans for today, this place is on the outside edge of your middle circle. Follow the route we talked about for today. When you get to the T-intersection at the lake, go left instead of right. The road goes east a bit, then starts to wind up through some rolling hills. Then it flattens out. When it gets flat, watch for a road going off to the left again. Northerly towards the tree line. It'll be about a mile or so from the road before you come to a clearing, where you'll have to park the truck. Leave a note on the dash, saying Smythens A21-12. That identifies you and your vehicle as being there because we gave you directions. There's a rough path directly across from the road entrance to the clearing. Follow that trail to get you to where you need to be."

"Dang it, Gord, you know darned well I'm going to change my plans and go there! What's so important there that you think I need to see? Are you sure you don't want to come along?"

"Not telling, and yes. Eileen and I talked about not sending you to this place. Be better to take you there ourselves, but last night's guests leave this morning, and there is another couple coming tonight. Too much to do here to be gadabouting around the country. You go and have fun. Take lots of pictures and write lots of notes. Dinner will be at 6:30 tonight, if you think you want to join us."

"Thank you. You two are the best!"

She laughed when she saw that the sun had not waited for her to take pictures. *Oh well,* she thought, *there'll be other mornings.* With the hastily written directions laying on the seat beside her, she started her truck and waved goodbye to Gord. The drive to the main road wasn't long, and Brandi turned south and started her journey to the unknown destination.

A few miles down the road, she stopped at the roadside pull-out she'd noticed the day when they had gone to town. She ate the muffin, drank some coffee, and enjoyed what was left of the sun coming up. She read the directions Gord had given her, re-writing the scribbled directions into point form to give them some clarity before continuing on her journey. Sitting looking at the paper, coming to terms with the challenge of the diversion from her original plans for the day was an exciting thought.

"This feels right!" She laughed. "Talking to yourself again, girl!"

Happy she hadn't missed anything from Gord's directions, except the sunrise, Brandi pulled back onto the road and started towards the lake. She figured, from reading the map, that she should be at the T in about an hour and a half.

The lake was about half an hour away. When it first came into view the sun sparkles on the water erupted through the trees.

"What a sight! Can't imagine how the early settlers reacted when they saw this view."

According to Gord, there was a day-use area less than a mile from where she needed to turn left. It was a good place to re-read the instructions for the next part of this trip, see if she had cell service, and try to reach Pete if she did.

"Well, Pete, I hope you are getting my messages and are hot on the trail of finding information. Looks like I'll have cell service for a while today, so if you get this, give me a call back, please."

She wondered if this man, who had been so helpful in the past, was now avoiding her. The next call was to Marnee at The Bakery. Maybe she could shed some light on the elusive Mr. Pete Noll.

"The Bakery, how can I help you today?"

"Marnee, it's Brandi."

"Well, hello stranger. Pete and I were just talking about you."

"He's there!"

"No, just left. Stopped by to pick up some coffee and a sandwich to go. Said he had some place to be and would be gone for a few days."

"Dang it, I've been trying to reach him."

"Well, that won't happen. His phone cratered and he's waiting on a new one to be delivered. Says it was only a matter of time, since the old one was beyond its prime. He'll check in with me when he can, or so he says."

Brandi could hear the bell above the door in the shop tinkling.

"I'll let you go, Marnee. I'll be home in a couple of days. Thanks for the information on Pete and his phone. I'll quit thinking he doesn't want to talk to me." She ended the conversation with a laugh.

Driving east, true to Gord's directions, the road was taking Brandi through some rolling hills. She didn't know how long it would be until she would reach the plateau at the top and was quite content taking her time while she enjoyed the scenery.

The day was still early, and she took the opportunity to stop every so often and take pictures and write in her notebook. Brandi didn't miss the hubbub and goings on happening in Notclin. It was quiet here. Peaceful. A place where the mind relaxed without too much energy.

One minute she was winding up through the open range, and the next she was on a flat piece of ground that went on forever.

"Holy!" was all she could say. Her mind racing in a hundred different directions as she pulled to the side of the road to take in the vast space in front of her. Trees were visible on the northern side, telling her that somewhere amongst them was her destination. Taking her camera, she walked along the ditch, taking pictures and absorbing the sight.

She wondered how soon the road to the left was going to appear. Gord hadn't told her that, only that it would take her in a northerly direction. It was almost noon by the look of the sun in the sky, and her thoughts already had her at the clearing where she would leave the truck before walking the final leg of the trip.

Brandi couldn't help but stare out her front window in awe at the never-ending pastureland. She was so absorbed in the scenery that she almost missed the two overgrown tracks leaving the main road and disappearing into the grassland before her.

"I sure hope this is it."

The trail didn't look like anyone had used it in quite a while, and it wasn't too long until the road disappeared. All she could see in front of her was prairie grasses and dirt patches. Panicked, Brandi stopped. Had she turned off the main road too soon? Had she just lost the trail, and now needed to back up and start over?

Getting out of the truck, she slowly looked around, hoping to see something that resembled a road. There was not an encouraging answer in sight. Remembering she had her field glasses with her, she dug them out from behind the seat. She scanned the trees, looking for the entrance to where the clearing was supposed to be. Nothing. She climbed into the back of her truck to have a better look.

"Is that bear scratch or a blaze on that tree?" she asked herself. "Only one way to find out."

Jumping out of the truck box and back in the cab, Brandi headed towards the spot she thought she'd seen the marks on the trees, stopping at about the halfway point to have another look through the field glasses. Sure enough, it was a blaze mark.

"That better be the road entrance to the clearing."

At the edge of the trees, she stopped. She had to be certain the marks were where she needed to be, and that there was a road.

"Those marks are definitely not bear scratch," she muttered, pushing some branches out of the way to have a look at the ground.

Frustrated at herself for not asking more questions of Gord before she left, she turned to go back to the truck. She would have her lunch and then head for her originally planned destination. It wasn't that late, and she'd call the Smythens to tell them she would not be back until later in the evening.

It was only a few steps towards the truck when the old feeling of not being alone settled over her. Like the other times it had happened, she was not afraid. She had learned that the feeling usually meant she needed to pay more attention—focus. It was as if she were being guided by the breeze that had come up, making her turn back toward the tree with the blaze on it.

Brandi stood staring at the tree. She had no idea what she was looking for until the wind parted the branches enough for her to see more blaze marks on trees further into the stand.

"There has to be a road. The marks wouldn't lie," she said, starting back to the trees.

This time she made her way to the second marked tree she had seen. There she could see what looked like an old wagon trail off to her left about fifteen feet away. Knowing the blazes had been made to mark an original walking trail, it made sense that the road had been established in an easier route through the trees.

Following the road she had uncovered, Brandi drove slowly into the trees, glancing at the odometer and trying to determine what 'about a mile' would be according to Gord's instructions. She laughed at the thought of having to back out of the trees, if she didn't come across the clearing soon.

The odd blaze was still visible off to her right, and the odometer had just rolled over a mile when she could see the brightness of the sun shining into an open area ahead. And then, she was there.

Stopping the truck, she couldn't believe she had found the spot. The clearing was about the size of an outdoor skating rink, with lots of room to turn around. She knew the importance of taking her bearings as soon as she hit the clearing. She carried plastic ribbon in her emergency bag, and decided to mark a tree by the road so as not to lose her direction.

After marking a tree, she walked straight across the opening to look for the trail-head Gord had told her about. This time, she found what she was looking for on the first try. Happy with herself, she went back to the truck to have lunch and gather up what she wanted to take with her.

Everything looked like it had fallen into place, and now it was time to make the final trek. She placed the paper on the dash with 'Smythens A21-12' written on it, slipped her backpack onto her shoulder, and started up the trail. She hadn't asked what she would find there or how far she needed to hike on the trail, and Gord hadn't offered that information. She had taken his word that it was someplace she needed to see.

She kept an eye out for animal sign, as she made her way farther into the trees. At one point, she thought she could hear running water and stopped to listen, only to see the tree leaves rustling overhead.

There were more blazed trees, and it made her feel good. As she hiked, she found it interesting that the trail seemed to be climbing. Facts she'd discovered in her research for the homestead article indicated that most pioneers built in sheltered areas that were close to water and good pasture ground. Walking through the trees, she mulled the expected stereotypical homestead location over in her mind, wondering what she was actually going to find.

She had been hiking for about ten minutes when the trail started to flatten out and the trees became sparse. She'd noticed deer tracks on the trail, but had seen no animals, wild or domestic, since she had turned off of the main road. Brandi was now certain she could hear water over the sound of the wind in the trees.

"It would be nice to splash some water on my face."

She was not prepared for what came into view. The trees gave way to a meadow filled with vibrant wild flowers. The grass was knee-deep and there was a creek running its length before disappearing into the trees at the other end. She couldn't see where the water came into the clearing, but off to her right, there were moss-covered rocks and what looked like parts of an old, rotted snake fence. She decided that would be the best place to start exploring.

Brandi's knowledge bank told her that a fence usually meant someone used to live close by or kept animals within close proximity, especially when there was fresh water near. There were no visible depressions in the ground, telling her where buildings might have been located. The grass would grow differently around any kind of foundation left behind. Going to a higher vantage point would let her see what was really going on in this meadow.

She reached the rocks and stopped to enjoy the cool water on her face. Bent down to creek level, Brandi identified wild watercress growing in the water along the bank—matted green, oval-shaped leaves with clusters of white flowers floating on the top of the clear pools of spring water. She pinched off a few leaves to chew on while she continued her tour.

Making her way to the top of the rocks, she was able to get a clear view of the meadow floor. The wind had died down, and so had the swaying of the grass. There were no visible dips or heaves in the land, and no indication that any kind of a garden or buildings had ever been here in the past.

Continuing to climb up the mossy, rock-encrusted hill, with its shards of rotted fence along both sides; again, she found no signs to say anyone had ever lived there. She couldn't figure out why the water had been fenced off on both sides.

Stopping close to the top of the hill, she took pictures of the meadow, the fence, and the creek.

Reaching the top of the hill, she found where the water made its entrance. Here, it was clear the fence had been built across the top of the opening in the ground where the spring emerged.

"So the fence was built to keep things from falling into the hole where the spring came out. Maybe to stop animals from wandering up the creek and not being able to get back down? Oh heck, what do I know?"

She sat down on a rock and looked out over the land. Writing, writing, and writing more, she couldn't seem to finish explaining what she was seeing and how it was making her feel.

The sun was starting to sink lower in the sky. With a shiver, she wondered how long she'd been sitting at the top of the hill. Standing to make her way down the trail, for some unknown reason, she decided to walk down by way of the other side of the creek. She shivered again, and looked around to see who or what might be there.

"Once again, it would seem I have company."

At the bottom of the hill, she turned to look back at where she had been. So many unanswered questions came to mind. She would be grilling Gord and Eileen for information on this place, including why they'd thought she needed to come here.

Crossing the creek, at a shallow spot near where the trail to her truck went into the trees, was the first time she had felt uncomfortable about the not-alone feeling. She looked around one more time to confirm that she was by herself before she started down the trail back to her vehicle. It was going to be almost dark when she got back to her truck, and she was thankful she had brought along a small flashlight in her backpack.

Leaning against the cab, she took off her wet hiking boots, changed her socks, and slipped on her running shoes. Using her flashlight to light up the trees behind the truck, she spotted the ribbon she'd tied in the tree earlier in the day. With darkness closing in fast, she was glad she had marked the road out of the clearing.

The distance to the open field seemed to take hours in the fading evening light. The headlights illuminated the flattened grass and small trees from the drive in, making for an easy route to follow out. If her bearings were right, she'd be able to head straight south and hit the main road on the flat at the top of the hills.

"One thing's certain, it sure looks a lot different in the dark."

~ 8 ~

The feeling of not being alone stayed with Brandi until she stopped at the lake to call the Smythens. She'd known that, as it got later, they would worry about her, and there was still an hour and a half of travel before she reached the B & B.

Eileen answered the phone, relieved to hear Brandi's voice. After making sure their guest was okay and on her way home, she busied herself in the kitchen putting together a light meal for when Brandi returned. It was the least she could do, she thought, after Gord had sent her to Spring Meadow alone.

The drive gave Brandi lots of time to process the day. She hadn't bothered to turn on the radio, enjoying the soothing silence as her thoughts kept returning again and again to the cool spring. Why had it really been fenced off? Why was there no sign of humans ever having lived there? What was it about the place that made her want to return, yet made her feel uneasy as well? What had she missed? Until she was able to talk to the Smythens, the questions would go unresolved.

"Maybe the pictures will tell me something," she said.

Driving back to the B & B from the lake, she conjured up a plan that started with getting the pictures downloaded before turning in for the night. Hopefully, Gord had been able to make arrangements for her to visit with the Longs tomorrow, so she could tour the meadow she had seen in her previous photos. Tomorrow night she would download the Longs' pictures, spend the next day going over the pictures from today, and any taken at the Longs. Stay one more night and then leave for home.

It sounded good in her mind, and now all she had to do was make sure it came together.

The information she had gathered from this trip gave her enough fuel to start an outline on her dream project. She hadn't realized until that moment that she was going to write about the whole experience. She would start with the dream clues, the subsequent location of the material items representing those clues, and figuring out what their introduction into her life meant. She still didn't know what they were saying to her, and because of this, she had the nagging thought that her research on the topic was far from over.

The rattle of the vehicle, when she drove over the cattle guard, brought her back to the present. She could see that the outside lights had been left on for her, and the kitchen light was on too. There was a strange vehicle in the yard, reminding Brandi that there were other guests besides herself.

"Oh well, a cup of tea and a snack is all I need. No visiting tonight."

Gord came outside to help her with her bags.

"Glad you made it back safe and sound. Eileen would have throttled me if anything happened to you."

"I'm here," Brandi replied. Her voice had a weary tone to it, and Gord noticed.

"You all right? You sound bushed."

"I guess I am. It's been a long day. I have a lot more questions that need to be answered. But first, how did you make out setting me up to see the Longs?"

"They've got stuff going on at their place over the next few days. They're hoping you'll be sticking around until next week sometime."

Walking towards the house with her host, she answered, "Can't stay that long. Got lots to do, and I need to get home to get at it." The disappointment in her voice was evident.

Brandi kept the rest of her disappointing thoughts to herself. She'd wanted to cover off all of her base notes in one trip, and now she would have to make a return trip to visit with the Longs.

She politely declined to sit with the Smythens and their other guests. They had finished the evening meal earlier, and were enjoying some of

Eileen's baked treats while they visited, waiting for Brandi to return. The Smythens had told them she was a writer, and they had wanted to meet her. After introductions were made, Brandi had excused herself. Eileen put her food on a tray and motioned for Gord to carry it downstairs.

"Do you want this out here or in your room?"

"This will be fine. I'm going to freshen up, and then I'll eat while I download the pictures from today."

"I'd like to see those, and I'm sure Eileen would too. Any chance you'd like to share with us tomorrow, or do you have other plans?"

"No plans now that I won't be going to the Longs, and yes, I would love to share them with you. I have questions."

"I don't doubt you do," he replied. "Our other guests will be gone in the morning by 8:00. We don't have anyone else booked for a few days, so after they leave, we could have a look with you."

Brandi was eager to get the pictures downloaded and review her notes. The pictures wouldn't take long. The notes she'd read over in bed.

"That sounds like a plan. Please tell Eileen I won't come up for the early breakfast with the other guests. If that's okay?"

"Not a problem, I'm sure she'll have some kind of a mid-morning snack planned."

Gord started to leave and then turned back.

"I shouldn't have sent you there on your own. Eileen wasn't too happy with me. It's not a bad place, but well, I think you know it has a life of its own."

Watching him leave the room, Brandi wondered what the heck he was talking about, until she remembered her feelings along the creek. *It's late; leave it alone,* she thought, *the story will eventually be told.*

After loading the pictures onto the computer and starting to review her notes, Brandi decided to write out a new game-plan. It was well after midnight when she turned the light out to fall asleep. Her mind continued to churn, looking for something to give her some answers and closure.

She had wanted to sleep in, but found herself awake soon after first light. She heard steps on the floor above her and surmised it was Gord up making coffee before leaving to do chores. Quietly, she slipped upstairs and filled her go-cup with coffee and took a muffin from the cake plate on the sideboard to go with the fruit she had in her room. This would be breakfast.

She shook her head in disbelief at the mess when she re-entered the room. She hadn't slept well. The bedding was askew and only some of her books and maps were on the bed. The rest had made it to the floor.

First things first, she thought. A shower, re-group, and then tackle the mess before her. Brandi could barely remember anything she'd done the night before. She was aware of how exhausted she'd been when she got into bed. Now she questioned herself as to why she had bothered to try to do any work at all.

Wearing her sweatsuit, and with her hair still in a towel, she picked up the papers strewn about the room. She was going to have to start from the beginning of yesterday and make her way to whatever point had put her to sleep. There was no other way to get a handle on the pile of material.

"Maybe it's a good thing I can't go to the Longs' today," she said to the messed up bed, while straightening the covers.

Today, she was resigned to work in the common area for as long as it took to get her mind back on track. That would give her enough time to see everything from yesterday with a fresh perspective. She looked at her watch; it was after 8:00, time to move everything out to the table, eat breakfast, and get started.

Deep in thought and munching an apple, Brandi was startled by Eileen's quiet voice.

"Would you like to come and join me upstairs? Our other guests have left, and Gord had to go back to the barn for something."

Brandi stood and smiled at the older woman.

"I'd like that," she answered. *So much for getting back to business,* she thought, pushing the papers aside to follow Eileen upstairs.

The two women sat at the kitchen table visiting. A carafe of coffee and a platter of freshly made Danishes, muffins, and banana bread were off to one side.

"Did you have a good day yesterday?"

"It was long and exhausting. It didn't sink in until I was showering this morning exactly how much the day had drained me."

"Mmm, that place seems to do that to a person."

"You've been there?"

"Gord and I go a few times a year by ourselves, and sometimes with guests who, over the years, have become friends. I wasn't happy when I found out he had given you directions to get there."

"Why?"

"People that don't know how to tell directions from what Mother Nature gives us, or aren't able to read a compass, can easily get turned around up there. They can lose their way."

"It didn't look like anyone had been there for a while. It's a beautiful place, but I was disappointed not to find signs of anyone ever having lived there. The only bit of history seems to be what's left of the snake fence in places along the creek."

"You didn't follow the creek to where it goes into the trees?"

"No, I climbed the rocks to the top of the hill where it looks like the water comes out of the ground."

Eileen stood and picked up the carafe.

"I'll make some fresh coffee and get a cup for Gord. He should be along any minute and will want to be in on the conversation."

Eileen had no sooner made the comment than Gord came into the mudroom from outside.

"I'll just wash up. Hope you didn't start without me," he said over the sound of the water running into the sink.

"Start what?" Eileen teased. "We're just about to have coffee and goodies. We wouldn't start that without you."

Listening to the couple's easy conversation made Brandi smile. *How could you not feel at home here?* she thought.

Gord was still drying his hands when he joined them at the table.

"Where are your manners, Gord?" Eileen whispered to her husband who looked questioning back at her.

"The towel!"

"Oh," he said. He draped the cloth over the back of his chair before sitting down.

Eileen shook her head, took the towel off the chair, and hung it up before reclaiming her seat. She poured coffee for everyone and passed the platter of pastries to Brandi.

"Bring me up to speed on what you've been yakking about, or have you two women been sitting here gossiping while I've been working?"

Brandi started to laugh. Eileen was trying hard to keep a straight face and give her husband a stern look at the same time. It didn't work. Soon all three of them were laughing. When they finally quieted, it was Brandi who spoke first, filling Gord in about her and Eileen's conversation.

"We were at the part where I climbed to where the creek comes out of the ground."

"So, did you go the other direction along the creek?"

"Eileen asked me that. No, I didn't. Should I have?"

"You saw where the creek went into the trees across the meadow?"

"Yes, but it wasn't as interesting at the time as it's become this morning."

"Had the meadow been grazed at all? Did you see any tracks?"

"No. Yes," Brandi replied.

"What?"

"I answered your questions."

Gord realized that she had indeed answered his questions, and with a slight guffaw, he asked, "What kind of tracks?"

"Deer, and to answer your next question, maybe a couple of days old."

This time Gord and Eileen both laughed.

"Good comeback," Eileen said, between giggles.

"So what's so important about going the other direction on the creek?"

"There is an old wagon road that comes into the meadow right about where the creek leaves it," Eileen said. "When the grass is grazed down, it's pretty easy to spot."

"But there are no markings in the meadow that would indicate the road crosses and meets up with the trail I came in on, or any road that might go back to the clearing where I left my truck."

"That's right; that road only leads to some old buildings down the hill a bit. It's like they used it to haul water from the spring to the homestead."

"Doesn't the creek go near the buildings?"

"Actually, it disappears back into the ground not long after it goes into the trees," said Gord.

"Holy!" Brandi said.

Gord continued with the history lesson. He explained that, for obvious reasons, the place was called Spring Meadow. He carried on with other facts that were common knowledge among the locals.

Brandi furiously wrote to keep up with him. When he stopped talking, she lifted her head and put down the pen, looking at both of the Smythens with a perplexed expression.

"I have a gazillion questions, but for starters, do you know the name of the original settlers, and are there any living relatives I could talk to?"

"The history book you were reading the other day says ground was broke by the Cedor family. The homestead itself hasn't been lived on or used for a long time. No one seems to know what happened to them," Eileen said. "Rumour has it, that it's owned by the same company that bought the old Shire place."

"I noticed when I read about the old Shire place that it included legal land titles, and in some cases, GPS coordinates. Will that be the same for this place?"

"Yes," answered the Smythens in unison.

Brandi looked at Gord across the table. "One other question. Why did you have me write Smythens A12-21 on a piece of paper and leave it on the dash?"

"Well, if anyone came across your truck, who was from around here, they would know you were connected to us."

"That's it?"

"It's private land, Brandi. Like the old Shire place, us locals keep an eye on it. Can you imagine what would happen to that meadow and spring if it became public knowledge? It would be ruined in no time. That creek never freezes up, and the land around it is used as winter range for some of the ranches in the area. The feed is always good, there's shelter in the trees, and with open water, you couldn't have a better place to have your stock."

Gord looked at his wife and reached for her hand.

"We have to trust that you will not share what you saw there with anyone."

"What? You are kidding me, right? Why didn't you tell me that before I went there? I'm a writer. Sharing unique and historical stuff is how I make my living."

"This time, you can't."

"That's why Eileen was angry at you, wasn't it? You sent me there without telling me I couldn't write about it!"

"That, and the fact that you were on your own up there."

The tone of Brandi's voice had risen. She was angry at these people she thought were her friends. She sat for a few seconds composing herself. That they had told her about the place because they *did* think of her as a friend helped to calm her.

"Well, for your information, I wasn't alone."

Neither of the Smythens said a word. They sat and stared at her, waiting for the words to come.

Brandi told them how she had not felt alone—how something or someone made her turn to see the second blaze farther into the trees. She relayed how she'd felt compelled to go down the other side of the creek and then uncomfortable when she decided to cross it to the trail-head, like there was something or someone there not wanting her to leave. She told them how it had been getting dark and she hadn't been afraid of losing her way. Finally she finished by telling her hosts that the feeling had not left her until she was at the lake and had called them.

"It was right to send her there," Gord said to his wife.

"I think so, too!" Brandi replied.

"What you have just told us should be reason enough not to go public."

"What I have told you is not the first time these feelings have happened," Brandi confessed.

"These places I have been to all have snippets of my dreams in them. It's like I am drawn to them. They confirm they are part of one of my dreams, or at least I think they are. The frustration is not knowing what any of it means, or why I am going to these specific sites."

The Smythens gag-request took a lot out of Brandi's excitement, and her voice quieted as she went on.

"I will give my word to both of you that, until I am one hundred percent certain what the drawing card is, I will not share any of my findings in writing that is to be published. I will continue to write and compile information privately, in hopes of finding answers and ultimately being able to take those answers public."

"Can't ask for any more than that, can we Eileen? The lady has given us her word."

It had been an intense two hours of conversation around the table. The discussion about Brandi's day at Spring Meadow had been both enlightening and mind numbing. Some questions were answered, but more were written on the pages before her.

"Now, how 'bout we look at the pictures you've been taking?"

It was the reprieve Brandi needed.

"I'll get my laptop."

Gord and Eileen sat for a moment in silence. They had never met someone like Brandi, a young lady full of life and conviction. They were happy to have made her acquaintance, to have her stay with them in their home, and to call her their friend.

~9~

Gord sat at the table while his wife busied herself in the kitchen.

"Did I see the fixings for biscuits on the counter when I came in?"

"You don't miss a thing, do you?" Eileen laughed at her husband. "I thought I'd make some baking-powder biscuits to go with the soup that's simmering. Eventually we'll have to break from looking at the pictures. You can take Brandi with you to check on the cows, and I'll make the biscuits while you're gone."

Brandi came into the kitchen overhearing the end of the Smythens' conversation.

"Do you need to be going somewhere, Gord? We can look at these later."

"Nope. We'll look at them now. In a bit, you and I can go for a drive while Eileen makes her grandma's biscuits to go with her famous beef-vegetable soup."

Brandi needed to tell the Smythens that she would be leaving in the morning. She had made the decision when she was in her room. She would return when Gord was able to set up the meeting with the Longs.

The idea of going through the pictures and then going for a drive appealed to Brandi. She'd been running flat-out the past few days, and the distraction of getting out of the house would be fun.

"I have already sorted and catalogued the day we went to town. There are just a few in the short-list file that I have questions about."

"Have you done anything with the Spring Meadow pictures yet?"

"No, we'll be seeing those for the first time together."

"So we're starting with the town-day pictures then," Gord said, as he moved to sit beside Brandi.

"This one," she said, bringing the first picture up onto the screen. "Can you tell me anything about it? I can't remember why I took it. It's so out of context with the other pictures before and after."

"Can you blow it up? It looks like there's something there." Gord pointed towards what looked like wood stacked at the edge of a grove of trees.

Brandi moved the mouse and manipulated the picture to make it larger. When she was finished, the reason she took the photo was right in front of her.

The weathered log pile was still neatly stacked. It looked like it was waiting for someone to come along to take it home to use in a long-forgotten wood stove or snake fence. The axe head that was stuck into the end of one of the logs was rusted, and the handle was darkened with age and the bits of algae growing on it.

"Ha! You know, we've been driving past that old log pile for a long time, and I never noticed that axe before. Did you, Eileen?"

Eileen walked behind the pair sitting at the table to have a better look at the picture before answering.

"No, can't say as I have. I guess you get used to seeing something, and you don't really see it. Looks like it's been there as long as the wood has."

Brandi was silently telling herself that this was one more clue from her dreams, and she needed to go there again.

"Can I pass this on my way home? Is it on private land?"

"That could be on your way home, depending on the road you take. It used to be privately owned. It's part of the open-grazing co-op now, and butts up against the forest reserve."

"Why is it there? The pile of wood."

Gord scratched his head, as if to be thinking what to tell her.

"Grandpa had a contract to cut and stack trees for a neighbour who had a mill. That was before the roads are where they are now, so I'm thinking that, if you looked around in the forest reserve on some of the old wagon roads that are out there, you might find more of those log piles."

Brandi could hardly believe what she was hearing. Her thoughts were careening around in her brain. New story-lines were forming. Future editorials about western heritage were formulating. She knew meeting the Smythens had not been happenstance. What was it that had brought her here to them? Something or someone needed their story to be told.

"This is an amazing story. I hope there will be a time I can sit with you and a tape recorder and have you recount your family's history."

Gord pushed his chair back from the table. "Why don't we take that drive now? I need to take salt blocks out to the cattle. We can look at the Spring Meadow pictures after we have some of that soup that's smelling so good."

"Sounds good," Brandi answered. "Is it okay for me to take my camera along?"

The afternoon had been a pleasant one for Brandi. She helped Gord deliver salt blocks to the cattle, was able to take some pictures, heard more local history lessons from her hosts, and ate the best soup and biscuits she could ever remember having.

The three of them had gone through the Spring Meadow pictures together. There were a few the Smythens had commented on. Brandi tagged the one showing where the spring water left the meadow and flowed into the trees. It would be a guide the next time she visited the site.

Since there were no road tracks that went across the meadow, not even a game trail, she had asked the Smythens about access to the Spring Meadow buildings.

Gord explained that there had been another road located farther east from where she had left the main road.

"About ten years ago, there was some pretty bad flooding in these parts. Roads were washed out. Bridges wrecked. Landscape changed. There was never an urgency to rebuild that road, because no one lived up there. Anyone who uses it to hold or pasture cattle knows about the trail I sent you in on. Like I said, a pretty place like that, it's just better not to make it easy for people to find," Gord said.

"You two have been wonderful about sharing your knowledge of the area and the people who live, and have lived, here. I am looking forward to coming back."

"You'll be leaving us tomorrow, you said?"

"I'm afraid so, Eileen. I have enough material and pictures to make some major headway on proposed articles I have sent to one of the magazines I do work for. I'd like to get an early start back, so the day isn't totally wasted with me behind the wheel of my truck."

"I'll plan to serve breakfast at 7:30. When will you come back to see us next?"

"That would depend on when it's convenient for the Longs to have me stop in to see them."

Gord got up from his chair. "I'll give them a call right now and see if I can get an answer for you."

"Eileen, is there a livable cabin or building at the Spring Meadow site?"

"One of the buildings has been used for shelter in past," she replied, "but I'm not sure what kind of shape it's in on the inside. Why do you ask?"

"I thought it might be worth staying overnight there and at the old Shire place. It would let me get the feel of the place to add to my story."

"I can't see why you couldn't. We'll check around after you leave to see if anyone has any objections. You might find yourself entertaining some of the locals who are in the area riding range."

Eileen and Brandi were laughing at that thought when Gord returned from making his call to the Long ranch.

"Every time I'm out of the room, you two end up laughing. You're starting to give me a complex."

Eileen explained their giggles and then asked, "What about the Longs?"

"Like they said the other day, next week would be okay for Brandi to stop by. Matter of fact, they asked us to come on Thursday and stay for dinner with them. Are you able to come back at the end of next week, Brandi? We have things we need to be doing in the early part of the week and guests arriving on the following Monday."

"I can't see why not. I'll confirm with you after I get home and see how full my answering machine is. Right now, I'd better get downstairs and pack up my stuff if I want to be on the road after breakfast. Thanks for setting things up with the Longs, Gord," Brandi said from the top of the stairs.

Arriving home early in the day, Brandi's plans to get started transferring and editing her notes to her laptop were the priority. Sitting in her office, staring out the window for more than a half an hour, try as she might, focus on the task at hand kept eluding her.

The last few days kept playing over and over in her mind, like an old movie except that this one was in full colour and action-packed. All it lacked was an ending.

Finally, she took her laptop out and plugged it in on her desk. The backpack was next. Brandi turned it upside down over the clear spot next to the computer. Paper, notes, pens, pencils, an apple, her go-cup, flashlight, compass, and a pair of dirty socks tumbled across the desk, looking for a resting place.

A sick feeling of fear froze her when she realized the notebook, with everything she had recorded while she had been away, was missing from the jumbled contents of her backpack. Closing her eyes, she took a deep breath.

"Think," she said to herself. "Where did you have it last?"

Retracing her steps from the previous night at the B & B was the easy part. The end result of her mind backtracking confirmed that she had not left it behind that morning when she packed up.

"What have I done with it?"

She made her way to the bedroom where her bag sat, unpacked, on the bed. *No time like now to put everything away,* she thought. Unzipping the bag, she hastily sorted through the contents. Still no sign of the notebook.

Picking up her keys from the dresser and mentally crossing her fingers, she slipped on her shoes and went out to her truck. Nothing. Panic was starting to take over. Back inside, she sat at the table, slowly and methodically going over every move she had made since leaving the Smythens' that morning.

She had come straight home, unloaded all her gear, and made a pot of coffee. The laptop and backpack were put in the office. Bag in the bedroom. Thermos and cooler cleaned out and put back into the storage area.

"What am I missing?" she said aloud. "Camera bag! Where's my camera bag?"

Brandi scrambled through the house, opening and closing doors. Room by room, she searched for the missing bag and notebook. She opened the last door and started to laugh. There they were, on the floor beside the bathtub.

Back in her office, she cleared away the mess from her backpack. The laptop sat ready, waiting for whatever she had in mind.

I might as well start from the beginning and just write everything out, she thought. The editing, additional research, pairing pictures, and her next trip agenda would come later. The rest of the afternoon was spent transferring her notes into files on her laptop. By early evening, she was ready to print off the first draft.

Leaving the typed pages for review until later, she decided to walk to The Bakery for her evening meal and a catch-up visit with Marnee. She'd need to remember not to talk about specific details of where she had been. It would be hard, but she had promised.

Marnee looked up from the vacant table she was setting when the bell over the door tinkled.

"Hello stranger." She welcomed her friend with a hug.

"I was going to sit and have some dinner. Care to join me? Chicken pot pie tonight."

"I'll take you up on that. Pretty quiet in here tonight. Actually, I noticed it was pretty quiet in town when I walked over."

"Mmmhmm. Turn the open sign off and lock the door. Then we can eat and chat without being interrupted."

Brandi did as she was asked, before getting a set of cutlery for herself. She poured two cups of coffee and took them back to the table to wait for Marnee to return with their dinner.

Sitting down across from Brandi, Marnee served the pies with warm, fresh bread.

"So what's been going on in our little one-horse town since I left?" Brandi asked, buttering a piece of bread.

The two ladies spent the evening talking about the happenings since she'd gone on her dream-research trip. As luck would have it, Marnee was more interested in the B & B, the hosts, and the food than about Brandi traipsing around old building sites. The convenient flow of conversation allowed Brandi to skirt topics she was hoping not to have to explain.

Brandi strolled home with thoughts of the draft of her story flitting in and out of her mind. Opening the door, she decided to leave it alone until morning. Instead, she would start an itinerary for her next trip to the Smythens'. She made tea, picked up her notebook from the office, and made her way down the hall to the bedroom. It had been another long day and being somewhere comfortable appealed to her in case she fell asleep.

Fluffing up the pillows behind her, the start of the upcoming trip agenda played out across the page. There would be almost a week to get organized before she would leave again.

Wanting to speak to Pete before returning to the Smythens', she'd asked Marnee if he was back. She had been disappointed to hear that he was away on one of his "Be back when I see you" trips, which meant he could be gone days or months. She'd forgotten to ask if his new phone had arrived before he'd left and scribbled a reminder in the top corner of the page to call Marnee and check. Brandi didn't want to do the research legwork on the old Shire place if he had already looked after it.

She turned the page of the notebook to continue her agenda planning. At the top she wrote the heading: Smythens/Long - Get it Done - Five Days/Three Nights. Underneath, she started writing down what she already knew was arranged or was planned to happen. Other one-line notes came next, outlining her wish list of things she hoped would transpire once arriving back at the Saddle Ridge B & B.

The return-stay reservations, starting Wednesday, had already been booked. Her plan was to leave early enough to take the back roads through the forestry reserve. She pencilled in other stops along the way, but checking out the old log pile with the rusted axe sticking out of it was the main goal. Gord had given her directions on how to get there, telling her it would not be a problem for her to look around, since the picture she had taken was open range on that side of the road.

Brandi started compiling several points she needed clarity on. Those she would go over with the Smythens when she arrived on Wednesday evening.

She wrote another reminder to herself to put her cowboy boots in the truck. The Longs had sent word that they might go to the meadow by horseback if she was up to it. She had grown up riding horses and knew she would do just fine.

The planning list was almost complete, other than a few things she would add over the next few days. Glancing at what had been written so far, she was happy with the result.

Brandi had been procrastinating on how she was going to deal with the thoughts of the dream clues that had been floating around in her head. She decided there was no time like the present to wade in and see what she came up with. Turning to a fresh sheet in her notebook, she wrote Compare Clues to Reality. *Ha! This ought to be good,* she thought.

She started with the first dream clue: the long meadow. There were two choices so far, Spring Meadow or the tip of the meadow she'd seen when they stopped for lunch on the Sky Hill Road. The latter was the one she hoped to visit with the Longs.

The clues in her dreams were not presented to her in any order, now that she had come in contact with some of the tangible results. Cold and pristine made her think about the cold creek at Spring Meadows and its pristine location. The hollyhocks she'd only read about in the paper. She hadn't seen any abundance of these flowers in real life, so she left the reality column blank.

The axe was next. Not able to confirm anything about it other than that there was one in a picture, she wondered how she would feel after the pending visit. Again, she left the reality side blank.

The feeling of not being alone intrigued her. She couldn't explain it, not even in her own words on the paper before her. She thought it was important, and here again she couldn't put her finger on the reason why. Under the reality side, she wrote the words Not To Worry.

Finished with the comparison and additions of more thoughts and informative notes, Brandi could see that she really wasn't that much further ahead than when she had left on her dream-research trip. Was she grasping at straws trying to figure out what the meanings of the dreams were? Were they just that, dreams?

She set the book on the nightstand and turned out the light. Tomorrow, as they say, would be another day.

~ 10 ~

Answering e-mails and telephone calls filled the morning. None was of great importance, other than the magazine agreeing to the proposal for the new series. They wanted a sit-down to talk outline, timeline, contract, and fee. She'd answered with nine words: "Awesome, we'll talk when I get back next week."

She looked down at her To Do/Take list she'd been writing while completing her office duties. There wasn't too much she needed to take, and even less she needed to do. Brandi smiled. Years of travelling around doing fieldwork for her writing had lists like this getting shorter and shorter.

In the kitchen, she was about to make something to eat when the phone rang. The familiar voice she heard was definitely not his voicemail.

"Hello."

"Hi there, where have you been hiding out?"

"I could ask you the same thing." He laughed.

"Are you in town or still out gallivanting around?"

"In town and going to The Bakery for some lunch. Why don't you meet me there, and we can talk about whatever it is that's so important?"

"That, I would enjoy. See you in half an hour."

Hanging up, she went back to her office for her laptop. She wanted to show Pete the places she had been and talk to him about the Shire place. Putting the computer and notebook in her backpack, she put on her jacket and left the house.

The bell tingling over the door announced her arrival. Looking to the corner where Pete always sat, she saw the table was still vacant.

"What brings you out today?"

"Your food, your coffee, seeing you," Brandi replied to the owner of The Bakery.

"In that order?" laughed Marnee.

"Oh, and the elusive Mr. Noll. Has he been in and left or just not shown up yet?"

"He hasn't been in yet. Go ahead and sit down," Marnee answered. "I'll bring you a coffee while you wait."

"Thanks. What are you cooking that smells so good?"

"Chili and garlic buns. Fresh batch of buns will be out of the oven about the time you two want to order lunch."

"How are my favourite ladies?" asked Pete, when he stepped through the door.

"Boy, now that's cupboard love if I ever heard it," laughed Marnee.

Laughing, he looked at Brandi. "What? No smart-aleck comment from you? Not perking on all eight?"

"I'm fine. I figured Marnee represented us both pretty well."

All three of them were laughing while Brandi and Pete made their way to the table, followed close behind by Marnee with their coffee.

Brandi could hardly contain herself; she had so many questions to ask Pete. Taking her laptop out of her backpack, she started grilling him.

"Did you find out anything about the Shire place? The one I called you about to see if you could locate who the owners are?"

"Nope."

"Nope! That's it, nope?"

"Yup."

Brandi was staring at the man on the other side of the table. She couldn't believe he would have nothing to tell her. He had been her go-to information guy when she had been working on her Western Homesteads piece. He'd introduced her to places she would have never known about. He had brought her tidbits of information accompanied by directions. Now he sat there telling her he had nothing.

"I thought you might have dug something up." Her voice was quiet, hiding her disappointment.

"I would have, but when all you give me is a place called the old Shire place, with no land co-ordinates, no name of the original owners, not even a general direction of where you were. Really nothing at all. How did you expect that I could do anything?"

Brandi knew he was right. She felt deflated. She'd been certain he would have answers for her. She contemplated not sharing what else she had found. He wanted facts and she still didn't have anything to substantiate where the dreams were leading her.

"Tell me, what did you squirrel out while you were away? In your last message, you sounded pretty pumped."

"I don't know where to begin. You've really knocked the wind out of my sails."

Pete leaned back and laughed at her. *For somebody so darned smart, she can be like a little kid sometimes,* he thought.

"Why don't you start with this old Shire place? For starters, why isn't it called just the Shire place? What's with the 'old' that you always put in front of it?"

"That I don't know. It's just what the locals call it, and I fell into the habit of doing the same thing. Even when I write it down, I write it that way. I do know who the original owners were, and why it was called the Shire place, though."

Brandi proceeded to tell Pete about the afternoon drive to town with the Smythens', their stop at the neighbours, who she was going to see in a few days, and the old Shire place.

He let her ramble about the days she had been away and her findings. He didn't look at all surprised when she told him about the occasions she felt she wasn't alone. She finally took a breath and reached to turn on her computer.

"I want to show you some pictures I took. Maybe they will give you some insight into what I have been doing, seeing, and revealing."

"Before you turn that thing on, why don't we have something to eat and talk some more about what you will be doing when you head out again?"

Pete waved at Marnee, letting her know they were ready for their food. He preferred to be done and gone before the bell ringing over the door announced the bustle of the after-school crowd and the take-out dinner rush.

Brandi couldn't put her finger on it, but she felt like Pete was avoiding looking at the pictures. *Then again,* she thought, *I have described them to a tee, so maybe he doesn't need to see them.*

They ate their chili and warm buns while they visited about the upcoming few days Brandi had planned. She was excited to stop by the old log pile to see if the axe was still there. She told him she wanted to nose around for anything else out of the ordinary that might point a finger in the direction of the answers she wanted so desperately to find.

Brandi explained she and the Smythens had been invited to the Longs. She hoped to interview them a bit to see if they fit into the criteria for her next series that had been approved. They'd suggested she come prepared to ride to the meadow she had seen the tip of from the Sky Hill Road.

"Brandi, what exactly are you researching? You started out looking for answers for your dream clues. Now I'm hearing you say you're interviewing for your next series. In between, I get the feeling you're trying to do some investigative reporting stuff that will blow the lid off of something."

"It's what I do, Pete. The dream clues have taken me to places I would have never gone just driving around the country. You're right; they have opened up a lot of questions I feel I need to dig into further. Maybe there is a story here, maybe not. As for my next series, I am excited about it. There are some definite possibilities for me to include some of the people I've met and some of the places I've been to. I was hoping you would consider consulting with me on my next series. It would be the same as when we worked together on the Western Homesteads feature."

"I would consider that, as long as you know that I am not always available."

"What exactly do you do when you disappear? Or is that none of my business?"

"You're right, it's none of your business."

"Okay, then I have one more question for you, and keep in mind I would like to ask for more information."

"You can ask. Doesn't mean I am going to answer you."

"How do you know Jessi Smalts?"

Pete's reaction to the question was to stand up, take some money out of his wallet, and set it on the table.

"That should cover lunch," he said, and walked out of the shop.

Brandi sat staring at the empty chair across the table. She never in a million years expected that response.

"What's with him?"

Pete's reaction surprised her. It dwelt on her mind a bit, until she decided to dismiss it as none of her business. She had more important things to take care of now that she was on her way back to the Smythens.

Driving through the trees on the old forestry road, Brandi felt the excitement building within her. The directions Gord had given her so far had been flawless. Already she had seen two stacks of grey, weathered logs. According to her own theory, and the odometer, the logs with the axe should be near the fence-line a few miles ahead.

Thinking about her surroundings, she didn't understand the need of a fence way out in the bush, and had stopped earlier to make a note to ask the Smythens about it.

Tight strings of barbed wire strung out into the trees from each side of the cattle guard was the landmark she had been looking for. From Gord's information, the road should soon intersect with another gravel road—the one they'd travelled on the way home the day they had gone to the old Shire place.

Eileen had explained it to be the scenic route. It was the one they took guests on to give them a different perspective of the back-country. It also gave them a chance to check fences and any livestock they might come across.

Brandi spotted the pile of logs off to her right. Pulling the truck off the road, she sat looking at the logs, wondering what kind of story it was going to tell her. The clock on the dash told her she had lots of time to explore before she was expected at her destination.

Her recorder in her pocket and camera in her hand, Brandi started towards the logs and the long-forgotten axe. She didn't get far before the feeling came to her that she wasn't alone. There had been a few deer tracks on the road while driving, but that didn't mean there wasn't some predator lurking nearby. There were no signs of bear scat, and the grass in the ditch and around the log pile hadn't been trampled down. Both good indicators that no animal, wild or domestic, had passed recently where she was walking.

She continued towards the logs, taking pictures from every angle. Interesting weathered wood grains combined with lichen and fungi. Tiny seedlings sprouted in the rotted wood at the bottom of the pile. History and life combined in one spot.

She turned her attention to the axe, capturing more pictures to get the effect of its importance and its loneliness in being left behind. Taking macro shots of the axe, she laughed. "You could be a character in a story all about you."

Brandi had been taking pictures for quite a while, and knew it was time to get going if she didn't want the Smythens sending out a search party to look for her. On her way back to the truck, she circled the logs in the opposite direction. Focusing on the trees and foliage around the logs, she spotted the marks on the poplar tree nearby. From where she was, the marks didn't look to be too old. Brandi hoped they were markings for a trail that might lead her to more history.

Walking nearer, the marks were not what she surmised. The bark had been rubbed to a shine, not stripped off. It was likely the result of deer or moose rubbing up against them in an attempt to remove their antlers. She'd always secretly wanted to find some shed when she was out doing research in the bush. Maybe today would be her lucky day.

There was no antlers laying on the ground by the rubbed tree, yet she couldn't explain why she felt compelled to walk farther into the bush, because there was no evidence the animal had rubbed on any other trees. There were no blaze marks. There was no trail. What was it she needed to see?

Walking from tree to tree, looking for more rub spots, she realized the last thing she wanted was to lose her bearings. Turning back towards the direction she had come, a shiny glint caught her eye through the trees. Watching for the reflection, she started back to where her vehicle was parked.

The outline of the logs was in view through the leaves when she stumbled over something sticking out of the ground. Trying to keep her balance, she grabbed at a nearby tree branch only to have it bend, taking her to the ground in a slow motion fall.

She lay face down in the grass, unhurt. Laughing at herself, she struggled to her knees, looking to see what she had tripped over. She was disappointed; it was nothing more than an old tree branch. From this kneeling position, she caught the glint of light again. It wasn't from her vehicle as she had first thought, and it looked like it was coming from across the road.

Up on her feet again, Brandi made her way to her truck, across the road, and into the trees. She kept looking behind her, trying to stay in line with where she had fallen. The shine through the bush was telling her she was going in the right direction. Finally, she saw the culprit that had been teasing her forward: the metal roof of a small cabin.

"Quite the cabin." She chuckled. "Wonder why they built it here."

A little let down at not finding anything more exciting, Brandi turned back toward the road. The sun was showing mid-afternoon, as was her watch. It was time to get a move on if she wanted to be at the B & B in time for dinner.

After making some quick notes, she started the truck and pulled back out onto the gravel road, heading in the direction of Saddle Ridge.

~ 11 ~

Gord and Eileen greeted her knock at the door. The welcome was reminiscent of a greeting for someone they hadn't seen for a long time, not just a week. They ushered her into the mudroom, where she took off her shoes, and Gord took her bags down the stairs to her room.

Aromas coming from the kitchen made Brandi's mouth water.

"I hope I didn't hold up your dinner."

Eileen patted her arm and gave her a reassuring smile.

"I've just finished making the salad, and the stew has been simmering in the slow cooker all afternoon. Gord asked if we could have apple pie for dessert, and it's almost ready to come out of the oven. So no, you didn't hold up dinner."

Walking into the kitchen, Gord joined them.

"Did you come by way of the old forestry reserve road?" he asked.

"I did. It took me little longer than I planned. I spent quite a while with the old axe and the log pile. Found some trees that had been used as antler rubs."

"Any shed?"

"Not fortunate enough to find any left behind. Maybe one day."

"You're lucky to know about those kinds of things," Eileen said. "There are lots of folks who wouldn't have a clue about what you came across."

"I stumbled across something else that was interesting too."

The Smythens looked at her with anticipation. Brandi told them about seeing the reflection and following it through the trees to the other side of the road.

"That cabin didn't look that old. Does someone live there? It didn't appear anyone was around."

"It's a line shack," Gord answered, moving away too place napkins on the table. "That road isn't travelled much except by locals, so not to many people know it exists."

"I would have never seen it, if it hadn't been for the sun reflecting off the metal roof. Did the co-op built it?"

Eileen and Gord exchanged glances. "No, it wasn't the co-op," Eileen said. "There's been an old cabin there for years. It was only every few weeks or so that anyone would have need to be in that area. Every so often, you'd hear about some range rider using it for an overnight camp, but that was it."

Eileen stopped to stir the stew and Gord carried on.

"The old building is still there, in behind the new one, beside the corrals."

"I didn't look around the back. Wish I did."

"It's a good piece of our history in this area, that old cabin. A story for another day."

Brandi's writing instincts did not miss his last comment.

"The new cabin was built a few years back. We figure whoever built it couldn't have done it alone. It was only about four weeks since riders had been through there and the new cabin was put up during that time."

"You're kidding," Brandi exclaimed. "No one noticed this going on?"

"Like Gord said, that road isn't travelled very much."

Gord had sat down at the table, leaning back in his chair with his hands behind his head. This position, Brandi had come to know, meant story time.

"The first bunch of riders that showed up after the new place was built thought maybe someone had bought the place and built themselves a shiny new cabin to live in. The boys were only stopping overnight and figured they'd stay in the old cabin out back. When they opened the door of the old place, there was nothing left inside."

"Nothing?"

"Nothing. Even the old stove was gone."

Brandi sat listening and wondering if Gord was pulling her leg or if this was a true story.

"What did they do?"

"Someone had left a note tacked to the wall saying everything they would need was next door. 'Enjoy it and leave it the way you found it.' It went on to say that the old cabin would be left standing to keep tack and equipment in."

"So it had to be someone who knows what goes on there—what the place was used for."

Brandi was making mental notes of what the Smythens were telling her.

"They were a little trepidatious about using the new place, but sure enough, the old wood stove was there, along with the dishes. New bunks had been built and the old table and chairs that were in the other building had been replaced."

Dishing up her plate, Brandi thought once again about how much local history and information she had gathered while sitting at the dining table of the Saddle Ridge B & B. She had known these people for a short time, and the freedom by which they shared their knowledge with her was humbling.

Setting down her fork, Brandi asked, "Why has there been a fence built out there in the middle of nowhere?"

"The fence marks the dividing line between the forestry reserve and deeded lands."

"But there are cattle grazing out there. I saw signs of them before I got to the cattle guard."

"That's true, but in order to use the forestry reserve for range, you have to have a permit. It's a three-year permit, and you have to fill out an application and have it approved before you let one cow eat one blade of grass. The application has to list all the brands that might be on any of the cattle that will be ranged there. You have to choose if it will be cow/calf pairs, heifers, or steers, or a mix. That is part of the formula that determines the A.U.M."

"Sounds like government alphabet soup. What exactly is A.U.M.? No, wait. Don't tell me yet. I think it's time I went and got something to record this conversation. I don't want to mess with the details when I try to remember it later."

Eileen had cleared away the dishes and the evening meal when Brandi returned with her tape recorder. The apple pie, coffee, and tea carafes were sitting on the sideboard waiting for the next course to be served.

"Do you mind if we postpone dessert until after Gord completes his agrology talk?"

"I'll go look after cleaning up in the kitchen while you two finish your discussion. Then we'll relax and have some pie."

Gord had assumed the story-telling pose again, letting Brandi know he was ready to carry on with his lesson.

Appreciative of the little machine on the table, when it came to details, she turned the recorder on. It was the most effective way to make sure the facts would then be accurate according to the person she was interviewing.

"A.U.M. is Animal Unit Months. It's a formula used to determine how many head of cattle are allowed depending on the size of the range. The range managers from the forestry work with the ranchers in keeping a close eye on the number usage, to make sure there is no over-grazing. Around here, the range is usually used in spring and summer. That allows pastures near home to get a good start before moving the cattle closer to wean calves and sort for fall shipping."

Gord stood from the table and walked towards the sideboard. The after-dinner information and question period had officially come to an end.

"Eileen, if you bring some plates and cutlery, I'll cut us all a piece of pie."

They spent the evening talking about what Brandi had been up to the past week. She told them all her notes were now transferred to her computer and that she was thrilled with what she had been able to compile. They all had a good laugh over the tale of the lost notebook and camera bag and where they were finally found.

Leaning forward in his chair, Gord yawned.

"Time to hit the hay. Tomorrow's going to be busy. We'll leave for the Longs' about mid-morning. They've arranged for a cold lunch at the cow camp at the meadow."

"We're taking food for the potluck dinner tomorrow night. I want to be up early to finish getting everything ready and packed up," Eileen added.

"Pot luck. I haven't heard that saying in a long time."

"The Longs decided to make a day of it. When that happens, all the neighbours coming contribute to the meal."

"I remember those kind of days were always a lot of fun." Brandi yawned. "Is there anything I can help you with in the morning, Eileen?"

"I don't think so, but that might change come morning." She chuckled.

Brandi stopped at the top of the stairs. "Goodnight you two, and thanks for the evening."

Brandi stretched and threw back the covers. She was certain it was after seven by the amount of foot traffic she was hearing on the kitchen floor overhead. She quickly showered and made her way to the upper floor to find Eileen hovering between two coolers placed strategically on the floor, each packed with delicious-looking food.

"Good morning."

Eileen jumped. "Oh Brandi! I didn't hear you come up. I hope I didn't wake you. I wanted to get this out of the way before I started the breakfast. Let me get you a cup of coffee."

Brandi hadn't known Eileen very long, but this was the first time she had seen the woman rattled.

"I can get my own coffee, Eileen. What can I do to help?"

Brandi walked to the counter where the coffee pot sat.

"Can I pour you a cup?" she asked the lady putting lids on the coolers.

"You are our guest; you aren't to be waiting on me!" Eileen grinned. "But I'd love you to pour me a cup."

The full cups were enjoyed only for a moment before the two women put them on the counter out of the way, so they could move the coolers to the mudroom. They would be left there until it was time to leave for the Longs'.

"Gord's not back from doing chores yet?"

"He'll be late. He's loading saddles in the trailer and deciding which of the horses to take for you two to ride." Eileen started to giggle. "You do ride horses, don't you? We just assumed you did."

"It's been a while, but yes, I ride. I brought my boots, just in case."

"Western or English?" Eileen asked, sobering up a bit.

"Western," Brandi replied.

Brandi went to the coffee pot for a refill, while she and Eileen continue to visit.

"How many people will be at the Longs' today? You alone are taking enough food to feed a threshing crew."

"They've decided it's time to move some cattle from the long meadow range to their home place. Other neighbours helped their riders gather yesterday and this morning. They'll be held in the corrals at the cow camp. We'll meet them there for lunch, and you and Gord can help trail the herd to the holding pens west of their home buildings. It'll take most of the afternoon for you to move them."

Having not answered Brandi's question about how many people were going to be there, Eileen continued.

"There will be ten or so riders, including you two. Some that have been helping this morning will load their horses at the cow camp and go home to pick up their families. I'll take our truck and trailer back to the Longs' and help the other women with final preparations for the pot luck. So to answer your question, there will be about thirty or so for dinner."

Moving to the other side of the kitchen, Eileen opened the fridge.

"Now let me get some breakfast on the table. I thought we could have something light, since we'll be eating when we meet up with the crew at the meadow. There's usually lots of sandwiches, pies, and fruit to choose from."

"That sounds good to me. I don't mean to sound like a cracked record, Eileen, but surely you have something I can do to help?"

"Since Gord isn't here to help set the table, would you mind looking after that?"

Brandi had prepared for the day at the Longs' the night before, by organizing the least amount of her belongings she felt she wanted with her. She'd brought a ball cap, a raincoat, a small saddlebag, and of course, her boots. She'd tie the coat to the back of her saddle in case the forecast changed.

Desperately wanting to capture as much of the day as possible, the notebook and camera needed to go along, but she had to be realistic about what she could and couldn't take on the back of a horse. The tape recorder would replace the notebook and the small video recorder would be the substitute for her camera. Both would fit nicely in the saddlebag. Her backpack was packed with her other equipment, which would be left with Eileen to take to the Longs'.

The Smythens were taking a garment bag with a change of clothes, and had offered its use to Brandi to include anything she would like to take along. There would be no shower after moving the cattle, but she could wash up and put on a fresh shirt. It wasn't going to be a fancy dress affair, that was for certain, but she still wanted to be presentable.

Brandi had a lot of time over the past week to reflect on what she wanted to accomplish on this day with the Longs. There were a few topics that needed to be addressed and answered. One was whether the meadow was part of her dreams, and the others included whether the Longs fit her criteria and would agree to be part of her next series.

According to Gord, the drive to the meadow would take about half an hour. The turn off was before they reached the gate to the Longs'. He explained that this route was more direct and there wasn't much sense going into the ranch yard and then out, because it added another fifteen minutes. The old wagon-trail shortcut would meet up with the ranch road near the entrance to the meadow.

~ 12 ~

Brandi helped Gord unload the horses, tying them in the shade near the holding pens. Some of the other riders, who had been gathering the yearlings, were looking after their horses and getting ready to head for home.

Moving the cattle from here to their destination would be looked after by Brandi, Gord, their host Graham Long, and a few other riders and their dogs.

Brandi quietly asked Gord if he minded if she saddled her own horse. He smiled and nodded. Brush in hand, she groomed her horse and placed the saddle blanket where it belonged. Making sure the blanket stayed straight, she lifted the saddle onto the horse's back, settling it snugly over the withers. The cinch and stirrup fell to the other side and Brandi ducked under the animal's neck to straighten out the gear. Happy with the results, she retraced her steps. Leaning under her horse's belly, she caught up the cinch hanging down on the other side. It didn't take her long to finish with the front cinch and buckle the back cinch in place.

The gelding stood patiently, waiting for her to tie the raincoat to the back of the saddle. Keeping the lead rope around her horse's neck, she took the halter off, replacing it with the bridle. She followed Gord's previous instructions to tie the halter onto the saddle.

Letting the horse smell her hand while she slipped the rein over his neck, Brandi patted his shoulder and led him into the open, away from the trees. After checking and tightening her cinch, she lifted her foot, slipped it into the stirrup, and swung up into the saddle. Gathering her reins in one hand, she turned her horse to face Gord.

"Where do you want me?"

"You'll ride with me for part of the way, until you get your stride. Then you can choose who you'd like to partner up with."

Brandi nodded, moving her horse next to Gord. It was then, for the first time since they arrived, that she was able to take in the expanse of their surroundings.

"Holy!" she murmured.

The sight before her felt familiar. Brandi was certain, without a doubt, that this was the meadow in her dreams. Her mind reeled with thoughts. She couldn't wait to start pushing the cattle towards their home. She was filled with anticipation to hear the stories about the land they were on. This was one experience Brandi would savour for a long time.

She tried to remember what Gord had told her about the meadow being deeded land or a lease. It was hard to tell from the cabin and corrals. They all looked to be in good repair, but so did the old Shire place and the cabin by the forestry reserve.

From the edge of the meadow, the old road followed a route through the trees, climbing to an open space of ground that provided a view back across the valley and the meadow. The awe-inspiring vista was surreal. The feeling that she had been here before was very real.

Brandi asked if she could lag back a bit to take some video. She was sure there would be no objections; however, common courtesy dictated she check.

Moving the yearlings was a good way to get used to the saddle again. The pace was slow and the cow dogs were doing most of the work. Brandi managed to get some footage of these four-legged cowhands showing off their expertise. They would dart in and nip at the heels of the cows, going here and there on a silent command or a whistle from their owners, and always returning to the rider they belonged to.

Pete had been the one to explain about cow dogs and how the best of them are like an extension of their owner. "They are, for the most part, monogamous," he'd said. "Not to say they don't like other people, but they prefer the person that feeds them, looks after them, and respects them."

Brandi had watched the dogs while the crew was having their lunch at the corrals. They had rested not far from their owners. When the rider stood, so did the dog. Sometimes a mere move of a finger would have the dog stay or be at the person's side in an instant. There was no playing or roughhousing with these animals. The odd pat on the head and a quiet word was all that was needed between the team.

Now out on the trail, the dogs showed exactly what they were made of and had been trained to do. Brandi remembered a line she'd read somewhere that was fitting to these animals and their work: poetry in motion.

The road was easy to follow, in and out of pockets of trees and rolling hills. It was clear that they had started their descent by the increased pace of the cattle. They knew where they were going and probably didn't need the help of the dogs or riders to get them there.

Through the last stand of trees, Brandi could see the ranch buildings. The road ahead led them off towards a fence-line and an open gate. Beyond was the creek and the new home for the yearlings. *An impressive sight; no wonder people love to live and work here,* she thought.

After settling the heifers and steers in the holding pen beside the home-ranch pasture, the riders turned towards the buildings. Across the field, a huge barn, outbuildings, and an old, well-kept, three-story house was in front of them. Fences painted, yard manicured, and a huge garden sprawled between the house and the barn.

"Talk about self-sustaining," Brandi said to no one in particular.

"Pardon?" asked Gord, who had ridden up beside her.

"I was just thinking out loud as to how self-sustainable this place is. The only things that are missing are chickens, pigs and milk cows."

"Behind the machinery shed," Gord pointed past the outbuildings. "That's where you'll find them."

"Really! So they have cattle for meat and milk, pigs for meat, chickens for eggs and more meat, and a huge garden for vegetables."

"At one time, there was a mill over on the creek where the grain they harvested was made into flour. That was a long time ago, though."

"This place and the family are steeped in history," Brandi said. "Is the old flour mill still standing? I would love to see it sometime and take some pictures. Might be the makings of a good story."

The riders reached the gate to the barn, and Graham moved his horse into position to open it. "Not much there anymore," the ranch's owner said, before moving his horse through the open gate, "but if Gord and Eileen aren't in a rush to leave after dinner, we could take a drive over there."

Graham stopped his horse near the water trough and stepped off. Loosening the cinch, he pointed to the far side of the barn.

"Gord, you two can put your horses in that corral. They'll have access to water and there's grass they can graze on. If you'd like to give them some grain, the bin is inside the door at the front of the barn."

"Thanks. We'll unsaddle at the horse trailer and then turn them out. They'll enjoy a good roll after today's outing," Gord replied.

"The wash house is open behind the house, if you want to clear a layer of dust off before we meet up with everyone out front."

Brandi was happy to hear her host's offer. She would get her bag from the truck when they unsaddled the horses. It would be nice to freshen up before they ate.

The go-ahead had been given for Brandi to ask questions of the guests, as long as she didn't get too personal. Not really knowing what Gord and Graham had meant by 'too personal', and not having a chance to clarify the statement, Brandi decided to wing it and hope for the best.

Standing on the covered veranda viewing the crowd, she concluded there had to be more than thirty people visiting on the large flower-lined yard. Some of the men and women she recognized from the rendezvous at the meadow. The rest she was going to have to introduce herself to, and hope no one shied away when she told them what she did for a living.

She thought it best to start with the people she'd met that morning. It would give her a chance to get the feel for these casual interview tactics before she ventured among the strangers scattered around the yard.

"Well, here goes nothing," she said, taking a step off her perch on the veranda.

"Ms. Westeron?"

The male voice behind her shoulder startled Brandi. She turned to see who had called her name only to find her face in the chest of a man.

"Sorry," she stammered, stepping back to give them both some space. "It's Brandi." She extended her hand. "And you are?"

His firm handshake and eye contact preceded his brief introduction. She thought she recognized him from the morning, and knew for sure when he spoke again.

"I'm Ross. I work for the Longs. One of their range riders."

"You helped gather the yearlings this morning."

Brandi couldn't help but wonder why this cowboy had approached her. She was aware that most would prefer to stay to themselves or talk with people they knew.

"I wanted to tell you I was impressed with you out there this afternoon. Not too many town folk know how to put a saddle on a horse, let alone know how to handle themselves around animals."

Brandi was surprised by his openness and his comments, but was courteous enough to say thank you.

Ross tipped his hat in acknowledgement and started to leave her. Brandi reached out to stop him.

"Ross, you obviously know who I am, if you know my last name, since I was introduced only by my first."

"Yes ma'am, I read your article in the *Homestead Life Quarterly*. Good read."

Brandi's mind was going in several directions. "Would you consider talking to me about what you do for a living and answering a few other questions?"

She contemplated the request she had just made. It was either going to be an untapped gold mine or a cave in.

"I guess I could do that. Mind if I get a cold beer first? Can I bring you one?"

"No thanks. Would it be okay if I walk with you, so we can talk?"

They strolled across the yard together, visiting about his job as a range rider. He talked easily about the profession he loved. He slid little bits of his personal history in without realizing he had done so. Places he had worked and visited, people he knew. Ross told her he owned his own place and ran a few head of cattle. The contracts he had riding range for the big outfits allowed him to graze his small herd with theirs.

Brandi listened intently, asking a few questions to prod him. He agreed she could use her tape recorder, which she held discreetly in her hand with the end tucked into her sleeve.

"Do you know any history about the cow camp where we were at today?"

Ross told her a few stories, saying he thought it was owned by some big company.

"It's like the old Shire place," he added. "We keep the corrals and cabin fixed up, but sometimes it just gets done."

She was now hearing the same thing from more than one person and a shiver ran down her spine.

"Any idea who's doing the fixing up, or the name of the company that owns the properties?"

"Nope, just gets done."

"Do you know if Spring Meadow is part of that group?"

"Have you been there?" he asked, avoiding her question.

"Yes. I didn't make it to where the old buildings are though. I wasn't aware they were there until later. I'm planning to go back in the next day or so to see what I can find."

"Pretty place," Ross continued. "It's got a feel about it."

"A feel?"

"Ya, you know, like you have company."

Brandi could not believe her ears. This man was telling her exactly what she had felt when she been at Spring Meadow. She opened her mouth to speak, but never got to say the words.

Graham and Joanne Long were standing on the top step of the veranda ringing the triangle to get everyone's attention. It was time to eat. Filling plates with an array of food that would put many a restaurant to shame, everyone made their way to the tables set out around the yard and the visiting continued. Brandi found Gord and Eileen sitting with the Longs.

"There you are. We saved you a place." Eileen waved at Brandi to join them.

Setting her overflowing plate on the table, Brandi sat down.

"I was speaking with a fellow by the name of Ross. I didn't get his last name and I don't see him, but he did say he works for you as a range rider."

"That would be Ross Harmel. He should still be here somewhere. Probably decided to eat in the shade behind the house."

"I'll check there after we've eaten. He was telling me about what he does and some other stuff I am interested in. Do you think he's the type that would let me take pictures and write about him?"

There were nods around the table that gave Brandi encouragement. She hoped there would be time to go looking for the cowboy before they took the drive to the old four mill.

Dinner finished, the cleanup was started, and everyone pitched in. The men cleared tables, stacking dishes near the tubs of hot water that had been brought from the washhouse. Some of the women washed and dried the dishes. Others wrapped the food, readying it to be taken home by those who had brought it. Brandi was both amazed and impressed with how everyone worked together to get the chores done. Her contribution was to help bring out the after-dinner refreshments and plates of baked goods, placing them on a long table for everyone to help themselves. People sat talking, rehashing the day, discussing local politics, and telling jokes. They were a large community of mostly non-related family.

There were not many rigs or people left in the yard. Brandi assumed most of them belonged to the ranch hands still visiting with each other before they headed to their respective bunkhouses or cow camps.

No one stayed late, and everyone thanked their hosts before leaving. Morning came early for these people and some still had chores to do before their day was over.

"Would you like to go to the flour mill?"

Brandi came back to earth with the words spoken to her from across the table.

"That, I would like. I'll go get my camera from the truck. Where should I meet you?"

"The washhouse."

Brandi made her way to where Eileen had parked their truck. On her way to the washhouse, she caught sight of Ross, waved, and decided to make a slight detour.

"Can we meet up over the next few days, before I go home?"

"Sure, I'll give you a call at Gord and Eileen's. You are staying with them, aren't you?"

"That would be great. Yes, that's where I am staying." She hurried off to where the two couples were waiting for her.

"Sorry to keep you waiting. I saw Ross and went to talk to him about meeting me before I go home."

"How'd that work out for you?" Gord winked.

"Gord!" The three women admonished him in unison.

The two men laughed and kept up the banter on their way to the vehicle.

"Tell me about the flour mill. When was it last used? Was it just for the ranch to use, or did others bring their grain here too?"

Her attempt to change the subject worked. Between Joanne and Graham, the Longs told the story about the mill.

They drove past the pen of yearlings, heading across the roadless pasture in the direction of a tall stand of poplar trees. Brandi continued with her questions. At one point, Eileen interrupted her to inquire about where she had gotten her knowledge on the subject.

"When I decided to write about western homesteads, my research took me to places that had different businesses attached to them. Some had bush mills and some had gristmills. Over the years, a few became boarding houses, and there were the odd ones that became homes of discreet companionship."

"Discreet companionship? Now, that's a genteel name for an old business." Eileen laughed. "Did your information only come from your research?"

"I talked to a lot of people who provided me with good, factual information. I used old land maps, land titles, and census documents to help me confirm or refute the data I'd gathered. I was lucky to have the help of a fellow who knows quite a bit about the history of some of the places I chose to write about. Unfortunately, I have since learned the Cedor Ranch should have been included in my work. It was one that never came out high on the radar at the time."

The truck came to a stop next to a slow-moving creek. The old building had long since seen better days, and there was no sign of the water wheel that would have been used. The five of them got out of the truck in silence. Brandi started taking pictures and talking into her tape recorder. She was captivated with the scene before her.

"This is an odd place for a mill," she said. "Normally they were built where the water is deep and the current is swift. Neither of those is visible here. Where's the wheel?"

Gord pointed towards the far side of the building. "At one time, the creek ran on the other side. That's where part of the old wheel is. I can remember my grandpa telling stories about coming here to get grain milled. This here, where the creek is now, was dry."

Graham continued with the story. "We talked a lot about bringing the mill back up to standard and using it again. Then we had a hellish spring flood that re-arranged everything, including where the creek was flowing. It took out the dams for the holding ponds on the other side and did quite a bit of damage to the wheel. The pasture we drove across was under three feet of water for the better part of a month."

"You never made an attempt to fix it up after the flood?"

"Not much sense. With the creek flowing on this side and the holding ponds gone, it would have been a lot of time and money to get things back the way they once were."

"Unfortunately, like so many of these old buildings you find, they have been neglected to a point of no return," added Joanne. "We've talked about making a cottage out of the remnants. The foundation is still good, as far as we can see. Maybe one day..." Her voice trailed off.

Brandi stood motionless, listening about the history and dreams that had been washed away by Mother Nature's wrath.

Deep inside, she was yelling and jumping up and down. There was no doubt in her mind that her next project was going to be a success, if she could persuade these two couples to having their family histories included.

~13~

Ross not calling didn't surprise Brandi. She'd track him down later when there was more time to continue the conversation started at the Longs'.

Brandi spoke at length with Eileen and Gord about the Cedor homestead. She wanted to glean as much information as she could about the place before going back to take pictures and gather research material.

Gord confirmed the old road was usable, but still not great to travel on. If she didn't like the look of the road when she got there, she could always turn around and go back in through the trail in the trees. Either way, the next day's outing would take her to her destination.

The early morning welcomed Brandi as she packed her equipment into her truck. She wanted to make the trip on her own, much to the dismay of the Smythens, especially Eileen, who insisted on preparing a lunch and extra snacks for her to take along. Gord made sure she had other emergency stores with her, just in case she got stuck, broke down, or had to stay out overnight. The cabin, he told her, was open and there should be plenty of firewood cut if she needed it. The attentiveness she was receiving from the couple made her smile. They had become like family in the past few weeks.

"I'll be okay. If you haven't heard from me by 10:00 p.m., I will be staying at the cabin. If you haven't heard from me by noon tomorrow, please come looking for me."

With a wave, she was on her way. Filled with anxious excitement over what she might uncover at the Cedor place, she made her way south to the familiar intersection at the lake before turning east. Noting her turn-off from last week's outing, she continued on to the road Gord had directed her to.

She stood in front of the old house. The hollyhocks were tall against the aged walls. Their blooms welcomed Brandi to their sanctuary. This, she knew, was the last link from her dreams, and it made her giggle. Now she could go home and wade through everything she had accumulated. All she could hope for was a result telling her why she had been drawn to some of the most beautiful and awe-inspiring landscapes, vistas wrapped around and intertwined with history—the opening pages to the lives of those who had made this home.

Happy with how the day had started, she spent the afternoon strolling through the trees on the old wagon road. It led her to the meadow, where she followed the creek to its hole in the rocks, where it disappeared into the ground below. Making her way back to the cabin across the yard from the house, Brandi made up her mind to stay the night. It seemed like something she needed to do, even though there was plenty of time to return to the Smythens'.

The moment she opened the cabin door and stepped inside, she knew she wasn't alone, but this time it was not her imagination causing the shiver to go down her spine. Across the room, a person stood in the shadows. There was a familiarity about the silhouette. The stance perhaps?

Somehow she'd missed the arrival of this intruder, or had he been there all along? Her mind was in a turmoil about what she should do. Her gut told her to leave. When the person spoke, the decision was made.

"What are you doing here?"

"H-holy!" she stammered, a little thrown by the scenario playing out in front of her.

Quickly, she gathered her wits and took charge of her thoughts.

"I could ask you the same question. As a matter of fact, how did you get here? I didn't see your rig or a horse. Just what the heck are you doing here?"

Shaken, confused, and baffled, Brandi started across the room towards Pete. Within a step of reaching him, the door she had somehow closed when she came in, opened. Swinging towards the sound, she saw a man's outline in the doorway.

"Pete?" the man asked. "You in here?"

Before Pete could answer, the voice continued. "You're here!"

By this time, Pete had come to stand beside Brandi.

"Better come in. We have some things the three of us need to discuss."

The three of us, thought Brandi. *How did it get from one person enjoying a day to three people needing to talk?*

"Who's that?" she whispered into Pete's shoulder.

"You've met."

Two strides into the room, Brandi knew Pete was right. It was Ross.

"You two know each other?"

"You could say that," both men answered.

Brandi knew that telling the Smythens she might not be back tonight was probably one of the best conversations she'd had in a while. She was certain that whatever was going to play out was not going to be done in an hour over coffee.

"Would you fellows mind if we went outside to have our talk? At least until I know what's going on. It would be a lot less claustrophobic."

Without answering, Ross turned around, leaving the other two to follow him out of the cabin.

"After you." Pete motioned for her to precede him through the open door.

Ross was leaning against Brandi's truck, waiting for the other two to settle on the step before he started to speak.

"Nice to see you again, Brandi. I left a message for you at Gord and Eileen's. They told me you were on your way here and might not be back until tomorrow."

"I take it you didn't come to meet with me. You came to warn Pete I was going to be here."

Ross nodded. "You didn't need to be involved. But now, I think it just might be a different matter."

"Are you two in some kind of trouble with the law?"

Pete stood and walked out into the yard. "Ross, I know we can trust her. Whatever we tell her will not leave this yard unless we say so."

Brandi didn't like what she was hearing. She dealt with people who gave her information based on anonymity, but this was taking it to another level. She did not want to be an accomplice to anything they might be up to.

"Pete, thank you for your vote of confidence, but I do not wish to put myself in a position where I might have to purger myself in a court of law. I think I'll be going now."

She got up from the step and started towards her truck. The two men started laughing.

Ross put a hand on the truck's door handle. "It's not that kind of legal problem. It's above board, but it does include lawyers. Whether you go or stay, that's up to you, but there is one thing you will agree to and remember." Ross paused, opening the door for her. "You never saw either one of us together, here or anywhere else. You will not tell anyone that we know each other."

Brandi stopped in her tracks. Her feet couldn't move. They had her full attention. "What am I getting myself into?" she mumbled. "Under those circumstances, gentlemen, I think I'd best stay and find out why."

"I can't stay long. I've got a truck coming tomorrow and cattle I need to finish sorting before it arrives," Ross said, closing the door he'd just opened.

"Not to worry, I stocked the fridge. If Brandi and I need to pull an all-nighter to bring her into the loop, we're good to go."

"Wait a minute," Brandi said. "If I'm not back at the Smythens' by noon tomorrow, they'll come looking for me."

"I'll call them when I get home. Tell them I've seen you and you're okay, and not to expect you until later tomorrow afternoon."

Ross, Pete, and Brandi each found a comfortable spot to sit. Brandi produced her tape recorder and started with a barrage of questions. Both men answered her with silent stares.

"Are you going to answer my questions?"

Pete reached for the tape recorder, shut it off, and put it in his pocket.

"We were serious when we told you no one can know Ross and I know each other. No notes, no tape recorder, and definitely no story!"

Brandi had been focused on the intrigue of the potential story. She'd heard the words they'd said to her, but chose to ignore them.

"Come on, you guys, it's my job! If you didn't want me to write about your little mystery, why did you ask me to stay?"

Ross rose from his spot. He wasn't as sure about this woman as Pete was. All he really knew about her was the article he had read, the few hours he had been in her company at the Longs', and that she was doing research on a story about dreams—or so Graham Long had told him.

Pete had mentioned her a few times over the years, and Ross chalked the involvement up to a passing fancy. He could now see there was more to it than that. Ross was confident it was a platonic relationship, and by the way they spoke to each other, there was definitely a mutual respect and admiration.

"All right, no tape recorder, no note taking, and no story—yet! I can live with that, if you two will give me exclusivity when you want this story to be told."

The two men knew they couldn't stop her without taking legal action, but they both preferred a hand-shake deal, and this looked like it was the best option for everyone. There was a quiet nod between them before Pete spoke.

"We can agree to that, providing you follow our rules on this journey we are going to take you on."

Brandi could see by the look on his face that he had something important to add.

"Brandi, there is a lot to lose if you screw us over. Ultimately there would be a lot of people affected, if you use bad judgment and decide to talk to anyone about this, let alone put something in print."

"I get the picture! What do you want from me? Perhaps a pinky swear would cinch the deal?" The giggle was stopped in her throat by the stern look she was getting.

Ross stepped towards her with his hand out. "A handshake would do just fine."

With the formalities of the handshakes out of the way, Brandi started to pace. It was a sign Pete knew meant her mind was trying to put some order to the chaos travelling around in her brain.

"How about if we start from the beginning?" Pete said. "There are some things you should know before we cut to the chase and the details."

"First, I want to know how you two know each other and have kept it from everyone in this country, including me."

"We're cousins, and that was pretty easy to keep under wraps since we have different last names."

Ross continued with Pete's introduction. "I have my own place, and I do work as a range rider for other outfits. It makes it easier for us to have eyes and ears on things, and keep each other up to speed about who is going to be where and when. That allows Pete to do the odd repair or build stuff without being detected. Since the locals don't ask too many questions, the cow camps get kept up and there is no problem of usage by the ranches in the area."

"Places? There is more than one? And why would you care if they are kept up?"

Pete took his hat off and ran his fingers through his dark hair. The next part of this story needed to be explained very carefully. There could be no doubt what was at stake when he was done.

"You have visited the old Shire place, the line shack next to the forestry reserve, Spring Meadow, the long meadow, and now here, the Cedor homestead."

"Ya, so? The Smythens and Ross told me they were all thought to be owned by some corporate conglomerate somewhere. One, I am assuming, that is eventually going to build condo-cities for people who want to play at ranching and have a place away from their homes in suburbia." Her voice was filled with disgust. "I wish there was a way I could stop that from happening. I have seen some awesome country out here, and it would be a shame to see it ploughed under and covered in cement."

Ross and Pete were both smiling at her. When she finally finished her rant, both were convinced, more than ever, that they now had their ace in the hole. It was Brandi.

"Well, here's the deal." Pete laughed. "There is a conglomerate, but this one's not out to do what you are thinking. It's out to preserve these land holdings and any others that come available. The problem is not the locals, it's the people out there working against us that want what you have just described."

Brandi did not miss the word 'us' in Pete's explanation. She was determined to get the full meaning of the word before she went back to the Smythens'.

"Pete, will you let me make notes, if I leave them with you when I go? I need to work this through on paper. Get my brain around what is going on and needs to be done."

"Sure, as long as you leave them with one of us, write your heart out."

Brandi got her notebook out of the truck and started scribbling on the paper. She took her time, making sure she didn't miss anything, from the time she arrived to the last bit of conversation. When she was done, she looked up. Her brow was furrowed and she was chewing on her pen. She had included a quick list of questions she wanted answered before Ross left them.

"Let's make sure I have this right," she said, starting to read. Pete and Ross answered the questions and added more information for clarity.

"I have to get going," Ross said. "It'll almost be dark when I get home."

"Do you want me to come with you and help sort?" said Pete.

"And leave Brandi here alone? Ha! No way I'm going to be held responsible for what she might do, or what might happen to her while we're away. Gord and Eileen would have my neck if I called them to tell them she was okay and she wasn't. At least if you stay here, you can keep an eye on her."

"Go help Ross if you want. Nothing's going to happen."

"No, he's right. I'll stay. Besides, he's sorted cows in the dark before. He's pretty good at it." Pete laughed.

"I'll be back tomorrow after the cattle-liner leaves. Don't stay up all night yakking."

Ross walked towards the back of the barn. It wasn't long before his truck pulled out from the shadow of the building and left the clearing by way of the road Brandi had arrived on.

The dust from Ross's truck was the only clue he had been there. Brandi and Pete stood in silence in front of the cabin. Neither knew where to start, yet both knew the story and its sordid details would be told before the end of a new day.

"How about we have something to eat before we get mired down with the particulars?"

"I think that's a great idea. I'll get what Eileen sent with me. We can share."

"We'll add it to what I brought this morning. Didn't expect any company, so it's a little on the bare side. Just basic camp food."

"No need to apologize. By the way, how'd you get here?"

"My truck's in the old equipment shed at the edge of the clearing." He pointed in the direction Ross had gone. "You know, out of sight, out of mind."

"So is this where you go when you leave town, or am I getting too personal?"

Pete laughed at her. "Girl, that has never stopped you in the past. Yes, Ross sends word about which cow camp or line shack might need repairs, and how long it should be without people. I schedule my time accordingly or I come here."

"Have you ever been caught? You know, by any of the range riders while you're fixing stuff up."

"Oh, a few hands have ridden through. I keep my head down and no one sees my rig, so I pretty much get away with what I'm doing. Like Ross says, the locals don't ask too many questions. The feedback he gets from the cowboys that have seen me is simple: They're just glad someone else is pounding nails so they can tend to what they like to do. You know, ride the range and look after cattle. Most think I work for some other outfit."

Brandi was amazed at the things she was finding out about her friend. She never dreamed he would be involved in something like this. He was certainly a man of mystery and many talents.

With dinner and the dishes out of the way, Brandi and Pete settled at the table with a cup of coffee and cookies from the care bag Eileen had sent.

"Pete, what the hell is all this about? You don't want to be known, yet you're in the know about a company trying to preserve huge tracts of land."

An audible sigh escaped from Pete's lips. "I keep thinking that I don't know where to begin. If I start at the beginning, we could be here a week. If I jump into the middle, there will be a lot of holes you are going to ask about."

Brandi got up to retrieve her notebook. She quickly read over what she'd previously written, and in doing so, she was able to take the lead.

Her writing instincts told her she needed to know the whole story, starting from the beginning. She'd come to terms with the fact Pete and Ross were cousins, but it also left a void in the story. This is where she started her inquisition.

Pete talked and she took notes. Every so often, Brandi prompted him with a new question or thought that came to mind. It didn't take long for the facts to fall into place.

Ross and Pete were equal partners of a company that owned the Cedor Ranch. They had both gone to university after high school. Ross had a degree in business and Pete in accounting with aspirations of becoming a lawyer. Ross had returned to do what he loved, ranching, and Pete had moved away to pursue his career and continue his schooling. His life away had ended on the day Ross called to tell him he was needed. Ross had been approached to sell the ranch. The whole issue went deeper, because they had never mentioned to anyone their affiliation to the property. That was when Pete had permanently moved back to the area.

They had done their due diligence and discovered, somewhere in the local land-registries office, that someone was feeding information to the same company that had approached Ross. It appeared confidential registry information, about several old homesteads in the area, had been used to try to acquire those properties. Some of the properties were still in use and some were like theirs and the old Shire place. They had yet to find out for sure who was behind the information leaks or who was ultimately getting the information. They needed to prove it was happening before some important range land was scooped up by people who would turn it into something else.

Brandi and Pete were sitting in the semi-darkness of the day's end, so engrossed in the fact-finding mission that they had ignored the onset of nightfall.

Pete looked across the table at the lady making notes. "If you light the lanterns, I'll bring in some wood and start a fire in the fireplace."

"Sounds like a plan."

~H~

The lanterns looked to be from another era, which didn't surprise Brandi. They were full of oil and the wicks were ready to be lit. She removed the chimney, turned the wick up, and lit a match to ignite the wick. She let it burn until the black smoke quit, turned the wick down, and replaced the chimney. She carried one lantern to the table and moved the other to a shelf near the cook-stove.

"You ready to keep going?"

"Sure. Do you want something to drink? Coffee, tea, water, beer?" he asked, placing another log on the fire.

"You have beer?"

"No, just thought I would throw it out there. You'll seldom find beer or liquor at any of these cow camps, unless there's a branding going on. Then it's not until everything is done."

Brandi smiled and nodded, remembering bits of conversation they'd had last year, when he'd provided her with stories about some of the traditions she'd used in the homestead article.

"I'll just have some water and some more of Eileen's baking. You?"

"Can't turn down her baking! Let's sit over here by the fireplace. Is there enough light for you to make notes?"

"The cabin's not that big. With two lamps and the fireplace, the light will be fine."

They sat with the cookies and brownies between them and continued with the task they'd started. Brandi decided to open the next stage of fact-finding with a sixty-four dollar question.

"Both the Smythens and the Longs have told me that the old Shire place, this place, the cabin up by the forestry reserve, and the long meadow are owned by some conglomerate. You wouldn't know who or what that company is, would you?"

Brandi was almost certain what the answer to her question was going to be, but she needed confirmation.

Pete sat staring into the flames, nodding.

"Ross and I, or rather, our company, own all of the places you mentioned. There are a few more too, and more we are working on owning."

"Holy! Why? How?"

"The how really doesn't matter. The why is because we wanted to make sure some unscrupulous persons would not get ahold of them. We worked in the opposite direction once Ross was approached. We knew if we didn't act fast, we would lose the opportunity. We had the ace, because Ross is all over this part of the country and no one was any the wiser. We made sure the transactions happened through another company we have across the country."

Pete continued to tell her how they had been able to anonymously acquire the lands, until recently. He explained that, while in discussion for a purchase of a quarter section, Ross was informed that one of the family members, who co-owned the property, had been contacted by another party. The offer of more money from someone unknown had seen Ross's purchase put on hold. The family member assumed Ross was trying to purchase the property for himself. They'd agreed to meet and talk things through, and the original deal was salvaged.

"That gave us our first lead as to who was behind the condo-city company."

"Were you given a name?"

"Yes, and a description. It fit the person Ross had dealt with at the registry office. He tried to read her name tag, but you know how that goes, when a guy is staring at a woman's chest." He finished with a laugh.

"Why didn't he just ask her, or ask around, or ask at the registry office?"

"No! There is too much at stake for us to go asking specifics like that. You, on the other hand, would be able to get all kinds of information without pointing fingers at her, or us."

"And what, pray tell, am I looking to find out, besides confirming her name?"

"We need to know who she works for besides the registry office. If we have that information, we can delve into their company and see what it is they're all about. Why they're so hep on buying up these tracts of land. We all assume they want to build condo cities, but maybe that isn't it at all. If she's the mole, she needs to be brought to justice. What she is doing is not legal, in my opinion."

Brandi had run out of blank sheets of paper in her notebook. She stood up, stretched, and announced that she was going to the truck for another book to write in. She was aware Pete had followed her and was standing in the open doorway. Outside, Brandi shivered, not from being cold, but from the feeling she wasn't alone. The shiver was like the feeling she'd had during her first visit to Spring Meadow, and the numerous other times, including in her dreams.

Pete came and stood beside her, both of them marvelling at the expanse of black sky dotted with stars—close enough, in the imagination, to touch.

"Why don't we call it a night? We can talk more in the morning. I'll show you around the buildings. Let you experience some of the stuff that others never get to see. Meet the resident spirits. That kind of stuff."

"Spirits? You are teasing me, aren't you?"

"Remember what you told me about your dreams, and the times when you feel like you aren't alone? Have you felt it here?"

Brandi nodded, not knowing if Pete could actually see the movement in the darkness. She could feel it now. It was a warm, welcoming feeling. Had all the clues been meant to bring her here? Had her subconscious picked up on the need her friend had? One he couldn't ask outright for help with, without the risk of losing so much.

She had seen the long meadow. She had drunk from the cold creek. Viewed pristine pastures, located an old axe, and found hollyhocks in bloom at the homestead house across the yard. All of this had happened with the guidance of something or someone unknown. All of the clues had brought her here to Pete, Ross, and the Cedor homestead. Now she stood here with a comfortable feeling of being surrounded by a safe haven—a place that needed to be protected.

"Have you ever looked into it? The feeling? Has someone died here? Is there a cemetery or burial ground nearby? You know, all of the possibilities that go with the feeling there are spirits here?"

"No, we're used to it. Ross and I just laugh it off, make jokes about it. The locals, some that is, accept it but don't like to talk about it much."

"Gord and Eileen said they come here to visit."

"I think you will find that happens more than we know. Those who have lived in this part of the country all their lives are comfortable coming here and going to other homesteads. It brings back memories, and stories they've been told or maybe even lived. Makes them feel like they are not losing things important to them."

"Do you believe I had my dreams to eventually bring me here?"

"Anything's possible; it's what you believe in here that's important," he said, touching his hand to his chest.

"I think I might have been guided here to help you and Ross."

"Good. Then we'll make a plan and get started. Right now, it's late and we've had a lot stuffed into our brains today. Let's get some sleep and continue this in the morning. Did you bring anything in that care package Eileen packed you that goes with scrambled eggs and coffee?"

"As a matter of fact, yes. How about cinnamon buns?"

They walked back towards the cabin, both deep in their own thoughts of what tomorrow would bring.

The smell of coffee woke Brandi, adding to the disorientation of where she was. Hearing heavy footsteps coming towards her, she tried stretching in the confines of the sleeping bag, in an attempt to take some of the overnight kinks out of her body. The sound of Pete's voice brought her up to speed as to her whereabouts, and who was moving across the floor in the direction of the rustic bed she'd slept on.

"'Mornin', sleepy head."

Brandi rose up on one elbow before she answered.

"What time is it? Dang it, Pete, the sun isn't even up yet!"

"We've got things to do today. If we're going to get you back to the Smythens', we need to get to it."

Brandi groaned, flopped back down on the mattress, and thought how much simpler her life had been at this time yesterday.

"I dug around in Eileen's care package and found the cinnamon buns. They're in the warming oven. There's hot water in the kettle you can use to wash up. The coffee will be ready to pour as soon as you roll that lazy butt of yours out of the sack."

Pete turned and walked towards the door. "I'm going to get more wood."

She looked at the stack of wood beside the fireplace and wood stove and knew the wood excuse was Pete's way of giving her some privacy to get dressed. When she heard the sound of more wood being split, she laughed. *Giving me lots of time,* she thought. *What a gentleman.*

Ten minutes later, she was dressed and cracking eggs into the large cast-iron frying pan she'd found. She poured coffee into mugs, leaving them on the counter while she tended to scrambling the eggs.

Pete came through the door with an armful of wood. After stacking it in the wood box next to the stove, he picked up one of the mugs.

"We can dish up off the stove whenever you're ready."

Pete reached past her for the plates and took some utensils from a nearby drawer. Brandi retrieved the warmed cinnamon buns and dished up the eggs.

She wasn't conscious of how hungry she had been until she looked at her empty plate.

"Fresh air and a good night's sleep will do wonders for your appetite."

Taking the plates from the table, Pete lifted the coffee pot from the back of the old wood-burning stove.

"More coffee? It's too early to be outside, so how 'bout we talk some more and I'll answer the questions you've thought up while you were sleeping."

Brandi walked to the stove and let Pete pour her another coffee. She'd made sure there was enough hot water left in the kettle to wash the dishes, after checking to see if any water was heating in the reservoir of the old wood stove. She wasn't surprised to see it empty. With sporadic visitors, it was not a good idea to leave water in it when no one was around. It also took a continually hot fire in the stove to heat that much water.

She did have some questions for Pete. One in particular had been hanging on in her brain for a few weeks.

"Why did you leave The Bakery when I asked you about Jessi Smalts?"

There, it's out, she thought. Brandi held her breath, not knowing what kind of reaction she would get from him this time. She didn't know if Pete would do a repeat performance and leave her alone, or if he'd answer her question.

"She is an evil, conniving bitch!" He spat.

Brandi stared at Pete. She had never heard him speak like that about anyone. There was so much venom in his tone. She didn't know how to respond and didn't need to because Pete continued.

"You asked. You seem surprised. Ha! That's got to be a first. Brandi Westeron at a loss for words." He laughed.

All she could say was, "Go on."

Pete filled his cup and sat back down at the table. Even after he motioned for her to join him, Brandi stayed where she stood. The thought of taking notes crossed her mind. She didn't want to interrupt Pete by going for her notebook, but he took care of that for her.

"Grab your notebook. Come and sit down, and we will discuss what an upstanding citizen Ms. Smalts is!"

The caustic edge was still in his voice, and Brandi had the feeling she was going to get an earful. Not because she'd done anything wrong, but it would just be Pete's way of venting. He could finally get off his chest whatever it was this woman had done.

"Whoa! You really don't like her, do you?"

The look on Pete's face said it all. Brandi considered how she would move forward with the conversation. Definitely Ms. Smalts had rubbed Pete the wrong way. Now Brandi needed to find out if it was personal or otherwise.

"Those are pretty scathing words, Pete. What happened? She dump you?"

Brandi was taking a chance with the question. It was either going to blow up in her face or she would be at the start of something that needed to be dealt with. Either way, if she was going to work with this man she considered her friend, she had to know, for no other reason than he was her friend.

"I wish it were that simple," he answered quietly. "It's daylight, let's get outside. We can talk while I show you around."

Pete still had Brandi's tape recorder. Taking notes as they walked was not going to be easy. She grinned at the thought of just making him stop so she could write. Maybe then he would give her the tape recorder back.

"Let's start with the big house. You'll find it to your liking, I'm sure."

They walked side by side across the yard in the early morning light. They were talking about the weather, some of their friends, and Ross, when Brandi did a 180 and walked backwards to take in the view of the cabin.

"Why does the cabin have a fireplace? None of the others I've been to have one."

"This particular cabin was the original Cedor homestead house. The fireplace was where they cooked their meals. The forged brackets are still in place, and the hooks hang above the wood box. They don't get used very often. Sometimes when there's a crowd here gathering cattle, the women will put on a pot of baked beans or campfire biscuits while they're preparing other food in the cabin."

"The wood stove must have been quite a step up for those that settled here."

"It's been here as long as I can remember. I'm told it was brought in by wagon."

They neared the big house, and Brandi could see there had been some work done on the exterior.

"You been renovating this building too?"

"Some."

Pete walked past the big veranda towards the far side of the house, where he waited for Brandi to join him.

"We'll go in the back way."

Brandi thought it odd that they wouldn't go through the front door, but didn't question the decision. They rounded the back corner and Brandi instantly knew why he had brought her this way. The yard sloped down to a plateau that couldn't be seen from the front of the house or the cabin. She could see the visible outline of what looked to have been a huge garden at one time.

"Planning on doing some gardening?"

Pete smiled and informed her that it had crossed his mind, since it couldn't be seen unless you came to the back of the house.

"It would be easy for me to grow produce here, be a little self-sustainable. As it is now, I'm not going to turn any ground over that might draw attention to the fact that there's someone here on a regular basis."

Brandi stood listening to this man she thought she knew. Every word out of his mouth opened a new door to the inner workings of Pete Noll.

~ 15 ~

They walked back up the hill to the house, where Pete let them into what looked like it had once been a mudroom. She felt a shiver and mentioned it to Pete. He nodded, shrugged, and started into a big kitchen that had a lived-in look.

"Who lives here, Pete? This place is too clean and well-kept to not have someone staying here."

"When I'm here working on the place, it's easier for me to stay here than to stop what I'm doing, go to the cabin, light the fire, and cook myself something to eat. There's a little room over there that might have been for a hired woman back in the day. That's where I sleep."

He led the way through a big room Brandi assumed would have been the parlour. Through the window, they could see the sun was starting to peek over the trees onto the veranda.

"Let's sit out there and talk," she suggested.

Brandi was amazed by the character of the old Cedor house. Pete had been meticulous in his renovations and refurbishment of the inside of the building. He had spent time here as a youngster and had pictures and stories, all motivating him on his quest to bring the walls to life again.

She hated to ruin the mood with questions, but Brandi was up against her own deadline. She needed to be back at the Smythens' before dinnertime, and the drive time had to be factored in.

Sitting down on the top step, she leaned back against the massive log that was one of the several floor-to-ceiling posts supporting the veranda roof.

"Time," she said to Pete. "I'm running out of it, and you need to borrow some."

Pete agreed with her. He had to find time he and Ross didn't have. Even when they teamed up, there were never enough hours in the day for them to find out who wanted to take what was theirs, and why.

Again, Brandi read back her notes to him, on the off chance he'd remember a minute detail that should be included.

"And that takes us to Ms. Smalts."

Pete grimaced at the name, but nodded.

"Tell me what you know about her. Try to be rational with your story, rather than vindictive and hateful. I already know how you feel about her. Now I want to get to know her."

"Ross needed some documents notarized for a business deal he was working on. The last little while he had been using the registry office in town for other stuff. He figured since he didn't have time to sent the papers to our lawyers he'd just go there to get the legalities looked after. He was required to sign his full legal name on the document."

Brandi was knowledgeable about notaries and legal documents. What Pete was telling her was no surprise. She wanted him to get to the meat of the story and prodded him on.

"The only person that saw his name was the notary, Jessi Smalts. We're pretty sure she's the one that meets the description Ross was given when he was making the deal for the quarter section. She has to be the one passing the information onto the people who contacted Ross about selling the place."

Brandi looked at Pete with a puzzled look. "I still don't see the connection. How would she know Ross had anything to do with the Cedors?"

"Cedor is his middle name, just like mine. All of the male members of the family have Cedor somewhere in their name."

"Why did I not know this?"

Pete settled on the step opposite Brandi. In the time she had come to know him, she had never seen such a strained look on his face. He continued to talk, telling her of his unproven theory that Jessi Smalts was the only person who could tie their homestead land to Ross.

"What did Ross do with the papers?"

"Sent them to our other company for safe keeping until he needed them. Less than a week after he had been to have them notarized, he was contacted. No one, and I mean no one, had seen those documents at the registry other than Ross and Jessi Smalts!"

"Okay, let's suppose she is leaking information. It's possible, even plausible. She came to me saying I should be checking on the Cedor homestead, if I wanted an interesting story. She was surprised I hadn't included it in the *Homestead Life Quarterly* article. Told me I should check with my advisor."

"She knew who I was?"

"Well, your name was included in the article. P. C. Noll. No first name. No middle name. Easy enough for her to find information on. I'm thinking there are not many P. C. Noll's in the world."

"Actually, there are a few of us. It's only when you know what the C stands for do you get to find me. Maybe she did some hunting on her own. Maybe she went through a history book that explains how the Cedor name is carried on. I don't know how she knows!"

"You have no proof and you're grasping at straws, Pete. I can't confirm by what she said that she knew who you are. Nor can I confirm that what she was saying was anything other than I should have used the Cedor homestead in my article. So what if she thought I missed an opportunity."

"Don't you see, Brandi? She was playing you to see what you knew and how much information you would share."

"Pete! Get real!"

"Think about it. She called you and wouldn't leave her name. She knew where to find you. Where you liked to go to eat."

"You said yourself that was information any grade-school kid could track down."

"I need you to find out if she's our problem, and if she's working for others besides the registry office. I need you to find out why they want this land, and why they wanted the other lands we bought. Why is it every time Ross goes to make any kind of business deal that has paper crossing the desk of the registry office, someone else starts making offers? I'd bet my last dollar Jessi Smalts is in the middle of it all!"

Brandi sat staring out into the yard. Maybe Pete was right. Maybe Jessi Smalts knew a lot more than she had let on that day. Maybe she was in cahoots with whoever wanted this land. But why?

"What makes you think I can get that information?"

"It's what you do! Dig stuff up, do research, take pictures, then write about it to share with the world. Brandi, you have told me that time and time again. Ross and I could use your tenacity to get to the bottom of this. We need your help."

Her thoughts in turmoil and her brain in high gear, Brandi started her drive back to the Smythens'. The last thirty-six hours had been like a story from another dimension. One she couldn't repeat.

She had to make sure she did not mention Pete, yet it would be fine to say she had seen Ross. After all, he was to have called Eileen and Gord to let them know she was all right.

She could talk about the cabin and how she found it interesting that it had a fireplace. She'd be able to ask about that and see if they knew more about the history of the Cedor place. She would feel them out to see if they were aware of any more information about the so-called conglomerate that was buying up the old homesteads, and why.

She would have to play stupid. She could not show her hand on this one, yet she had to be able to depend on the people she had come to know. She had to use them, without them knowing, to be her eyes and ears.

The whole idea of not being able to go public with it angered Brandi. Dictated to keep quiet about Mother Nature's beauty and the want to keep it private was one thing, but to have people close to her throw the brakes on a perfectly legitimate story was quite another.

She had been tossed into the middle of their mayhem, all because she had stumbled onto Pete and Ross's story while looking for answers to her own questions. It was a story she would most likely not have come across if it hadn't been for the enticement she'd received from her dreams, and the pull to unearth their meaning from the unknown. Her quiet spirits.

It was not clearly defined in her mind how she had become so immersed in this silent battle. She'd been guided to some different yet similar land holdings. They were old homesteads with so much to tell, yet their stories were muzzled by the greed of someone unknown.

Brandi was determined to find a way to tell their stories and their history. For now, they sat in limbo. She would not jeopardize the facts she'd discovered, nor would she disrespect and undermine the friends she had made in her own quest to understand her dreams.

Up ahead, she could see the turn off to Saddle Ridge B & B road. This would be the last night Brandi would spend with the Smythens on this trip. Tomorrow, she would head for home to take on the anticipation of crushing the innuendo and uncovering the much-needed stories, characters, and especially the facts to put closure to the ordeal Pete and Ross were dealing with.

How to tackle this challenge? She was unsure. The two men had done a lot of leg work already. It would now be up to her to filter through their findings and squirrel out the details, including the first blip on the radar: Jessi Smalts.

That was, after all, what she did for a living.

The Quiet Spirits Glossary

A.U.M. - Annual Unit Months. The formula used to determine how many animals are allowed to graze on open-range and forest reserves.

Antler Rub - Marks on trees made by male deer, elk, and moose rubbing their forehead and antlers in an attempt to dislodge the antlers after the rutting season.

Bear Scratch - Jagged claw marks found on trees trunks. Made by bears reaching as far as they can up the trunks of trees to mark their territory.

Blaze - Long slice of bark taken from a tree trunk to mark a trail.

Bush Mill - Name for a mobile sawmill.

Cow Camp - A cabin with corrals placed strategically on a ranch range. A home away from home with easier access to check on and doctor cattle or other stock. Can be a full-time residence or used only as a summer camp or hunting camp in the fall. Not to be confused with a line shack.

Cupboard Love - A phrase used to describe an affectionate saying or act that results in receiving some type of gift in return.

Dovetail - Name for tapered end of a piece of wood/timber/log. Typically wider at its outside edge. Interlocks with corresponding notches in another piece of wood. A dovetail cut was/is used in building log buildings.

Drawing Card - Something that attracts a person's interest to an event or item.

Forest Reserve - Designated tracts of land owned by the government. Leased to ranchers to graze cattle and other stock.

Gristmill - A mill for grinding grain into flour.

Holding Pen - Corrals or pens where livestock is temporarily held prior to shipping to market, branding, or moving them to another location.

Line Shack - Small cabin located in out-of-the way places. Used as a place for cowhands to take refuge from the weather or stay overnight when range riding. No amenities.

Open Range - Public land open to anyone to graze stock.

Pot Luck - An event where everyone brings a food dish to share.

Prove Up - Public lands required the applying homesteader to make improvements to the land, i.e. clear part of the land, put a dwelling on it, produce a crop, or raise stock. Any or all requirements to be complete within a specific time frame in order to receive ownership of the land.

Range Rider - Historically, anyone employed to ride the range by horseback to check on stock, fences, and other holdings.

Scat - Wild animal poop (fecal dropping).

Shed - Antlers shed each year from male deer, moose, elk, etc.

Shire Horse - A British breed of draft horse.

Sideboard - A piece of furniture used for storage (cupboards and drawers). Often placed on the perimeter of a room. The surface can be used to serve food and refreshments. Cupboards and drawers can house such items as linens, china, etc.

Snake fence - Fencing made with logs/poles. Logs sitting across one another at the ends to form a zigzag pattern.

Wild Watercress - A perennial plant. Grows rapidly in aquatic environment, such as slow-moving waterways and natural springs. Small, oval leaves have a peppery taste. Small white flowers appear in spring, turning into pod seeds that are also edible.

Baking Powder Biscuits

This recipe has been in our family for a long time. The only thing I have to say about the preparation is don't overwork the dough.

- 2 cups of flour
- 4 teaspoons of baking powder
- 1 teaspoon of salt
- 1/4 cup of shortening
- 1 cup of milk

Mix together flour, baking powder, and salt. Cut in shortening. Use your hands to blend to a fine crumb consistency.

Make a well in the middle and slowly add milk.

Stir dough vigorously until it comes away from the sides.

Turn dough onto a lightly floured board and softly knead for a few minutes. The dough should not be sticky.

Pat or roll out to desired thickness - 1/2" to 3/4" is good.

Use a knife or cookie-cutter to cut out shapes. Place on un-greased baking sheet.

Bake in a hot oven for 12-15 minutes until browned. That would be 400 F.

Makes 10-15 biscuits, depending on the size and shape you cut out.

Flour - The original recipe calls for flour and did not define it any further. We use all-purpose flour

Salt & Shortening - Called for in original recipe, we use salted butter or margarine and omit the salt.

Baking Sheet - We put ours in a cast-iron frying pan to bake in the oven.

"Capturing moments other
may never get to experience."

~ Ann Edall-Robson ~

Books by Ann Edall-Robson

Moon Rising: An Eclectic Collection of Works
The Quiet Spirits

From Our Home To Yours Series
From Our Home To Yours: Cookies
From Our Home To Yours: Cakes & Squares

My Canadian Backyard Series
Birds in my Canadian Backyard (Release Fall 2017)

Contributing Author Publications
Voice & Vision 2016 - Collaboration of visual and written artisans
Voice & Vision 2017 - Collaboration of visual and written artisans

Photography by Ann Edall-Robson
DAKATAMA™ Country Gifts

Follow Ann on Social Medial
Website: annedallrobson.com
Facebook: facebook.com/EdallRobson
Twitter: twitter.com/AnnEdallRobson

CPSIA information can be obtained
at www.ICGtesting.com
Printed in the USA
LVOW03s1927091117
555693LV00001B/1/P